"Because all ——
since I saw ——

As he stepped tow—— ——
He could see her pulse pounding in her throat, saw
the taut neediness of her body, knew her every
nerve ending was tingling just as his were.

She gave a small sigh. The familiarity of her scent
spun his head, and he glanced down as she laid a
hand against his chest and looked up at him, her
eyes wide. Her lips parted, and now he was no
more capable of stopping this momentum. It would
be simpler to stop breathing altogether.

One kiss—there could be no harm in that. A
bittersweet reminder of the past.

Then he did kiss her, and it felt gloriously familiar
and yet oh so new, and as she moaned, a fierce
satisfaction rocketed through him and he deepened
the intensity of the kiss, wanting to plunder the
sweetness of her lips.

Then they sprang apart, their ragged breaths
mingling as they stared at each other in mirrored
shock.

Dear Reader,

This book was written during turbulent times both globally and in my own life. As such, it was wonderful to escape into, and where better to escape to than to Sri Lanka? A sentiment not initially shared by my hero and heroine!

Matt and Zoe would rather be anywhere else—they haven't seen each other since the end of their brief ill-fated marriage. But now they are on an idyllic beach resort to celebrate Zoe's sister's wedding to Matt's best mate. And there is no escape!

And yet as they are thrown together against the backdrop of sun-dappled sand, turquoise skies and a vibrant Sri Lankan festival, they begin to remember why they fell for each other in the first place.

Could there be a happy ending this time? I hope you enjoy finding out.

Nina x

Second Chance in Sri Lanka

Nina Milne

H HARLEQUIN

Romance

Recycling programs
for this product may
not exist in your area.

ISBN-13: 978-1-335-40710-8

Second Chance in Sri Lanka

Copyright © 2022 by Nina Milne

For questions and comments about the quality of this book,
please contact us at CustomerService@Harlequin.com.

Harlequin Enterprises ULC
22 Adelaide St. West, 41st Floor
Toronto, Ontario M5H 4E3, Canada
www.Harlequin.com

Printed in U.S.A.

Nina Milne has always dreamed of writing for Harlequin Romance—ever since she played libraries with her mother's stacks of Harlequin romances as a child. On her way to this dream, Nina acquired an English degree, a hero of her own, three gorgeous children and—somehow!—an accountancy qualification. She lives in Brighton and has filled her house with stacks of books—her very own *real* library.

Books by Nina Milne

Harlequin Romance

The Casseveti Inheritance

Italian Escape with the CEO
Whisked Away by the Italian Tycoon
The Secret Casseveti Baby

A Crown by Christmas

Their Christmas Royal Wedding

Marooned with the Millionaire
Conveniently Wed to the Prince
Hired Girlfriend, Pregnant Fiancée?
Whisked Away by Her Millionaire Boss
Baby on the Tycoon's Doorstep

Visit the Author Profile page
at Harlequin.com for more titles.

To my family—you are all amazing!

Praise for
Nina Milne

CHAPTER ONE

ZOE STARED OUT of the villa window, focused on the scene, the peaceful, idyllic scene, focused so hard the vista blurred as she desperately tried to summon up a corresponding tranquillity.

After all, how hard could that be? Sand curved in a crescent of different-hued tones: honey and amber and the haze of absorbed sunlight. The blue of the ocean, a glorious swirl of azure and teal that stretched to the horizon, blended with the light turquoise of the sky. Palm trees fringed the landscape and the only sound was the caw and coo of the exotic birds that plumed this gorgeous bit of Sri Lanka.

But none of it made an iota of difference to the turbulence that had taken hold of her nerves. All because in the next hour or so she would see Matt again. The idea churned her stomach, accelerated her heart rate and turned the view from her window into an an-odyne tawdry souvenir postcard vista.

Get over it, Zoe.

This was not about her. It was about Beth, her much-loved older sister. Zoe was here in Sri Lanka to celebrate Beth's wedding to Dylan. It was simply unfortunate that Dylan's best friend and best man happened to be Matt Sutherland. Of course, if Matt and Dylan weren't friends Zoe would never have met Matt. Five years ago she had agreed to let her sister arrange a date, a single mojito; she had met Matt, the mojito had been followed by dinner and she'd fallen for him. Six months later she'd fallen pregnant and fallen into a hasty marriage.

Remembered pain struck, her miscarriage and the aftermath. She'd only been ten weeks pregnant, had known she wasn't 'safe' yet, but it hadn't made a difference to the pain she'd felt, at the loss of the potential life, the son or daughter she'd never now hold or know, or even feel kick in her womb.

'No particular reason,' the doctor had said in an attempt to reassure her. 'No reason not to try again.'

And Zoe had known that was what she wanted to do—she might not have planned to have a baby, but her pregnancy had given her a bone-deep knowledge that she wanted a family, wanted to be a parent, wanted the family life she'd never had herself.

But then she'd told Matt how she felt and that was when he'd dropped the bomb that had blown their short, ill-fated marriage up. Words that were etched on her brain, burnt there for ever.

I don't feel the same way, Zoe. I would have done the best I could to be a good father. But I don't want children.

The words had devastated her, made her feel as though everything was a lie.

Why didn't you say?

Because there wasn't any point. You were pregnant and I...

Thought you'd have to make the best of it.

Her voice had been small and tight as the cold hand of grief had touched her again.

I thought you wanted our baby, I thought... I did.

He'd made a helpless gesture with his hand.

And I am devastated we lost the baby. I swear it.

And she'd known he spoke truth; had witnessed the white face, the set expression, the storm of grief in his brown eyes.

But that doesn't mean I want to try for another one.

Zoe had known she couldn't live with a man who didn't want a family and so she'd left. Packed a bag, taken off travelling, decided to spend a few years honing her cooking skills abroad, before fulfilling her dream to open her own restaurant. So she'd taken jobs as waitress, kitchen assistant, worked her way up to chef status, and had just completed a six-month contract managing a restaurant in Switzerland to cover maternity leave.

She had put Matt out of her mind, a small sliver of her past, a blip, no more. After all, in truth, as his words had proved with such bleak clarity, they had barely known each other, their marriage a mistake. Even if she hadn't lost the baby, what real chance had they had? With hindsight the wedding had been a foolhardy venture, and yet, looking back, Zoe could recall the heady rush that had carried her away. Being with Matt had made her feel alive for the first time since Tom's death. Tom, her first doomed love. Together they had spun off the rails so far they hadn't seen tragedy bearing down on them. Tom had been so vital and alive and then he'd died, aged eighteen, of an accidental overdose.

So with Matt it had seemed almost as though fate had given her a chance to make up for the tragedy she felt responsible for.

Had gifted her an opportunity, to have a baby, have a real family, and she'd snatched at that chance. She'd wanted to give her baby a father who wanted to be there, and Matt's instant insistence on marriage had seemed proof of exactly that. And so she'd believed in the fairy-tale ending—oh, he'd never claimed to love her but that hadn't mattered. In truth she'd believed they could live happily ever after, had been carried away on a sweeping tide of attraction and illusory optimism, headed towards the dream where she would give her baby the perfect family she'd craved for herself. Well, that hadn't happened, and Matt had been consigned to history. A sliver of history.

Until today. When she had to acknowledge that the idea of seeing him had sent her into an out of proportion spin. She closed her eyes and started reciting spices in alphabetical order in her head. It would all be fine. It had to be. Beth had always been there for her and no way would she spoil the next few days that her sister had planned with such care.

Dylan's mum was from Sri Lanka and, though she had not been back for many years, she had always wanted Dylan to know and understand his heritage and so Beth and Dylan had decided to get married here, combine their wedding and honeymoon with the chance to spend time on Lavantivu, an island where his family had once lived.

They also decided they only wanted a small wedding with just close family and Matt in attendance and that they would like to spend time together before the ceremony. So they'd booked a few adjoining holiday houses on a beautiful small resort on Lavantivu for a week prior to the wedding and planned an itinerary of activities. Then the party would move to the city of Burati for the actual wedding, to be held in a luxurious hotel.

Today was arrival day and everyone was about to congregate for lunch in the central building that housed a large kitchen and dining area. Everyone except their parents. The all too familiar sense of anger, frustration and sadness ran through her. Neil and Joanna Trewallen had missed nearly every single one of their daughters' important life events, their lives dominated by the number of charitable causes they supported, one of which always needed them. In this case they had decided at the last minute not to attend as it would be hypocritical, given they were about to march for climate change.

So you see, darling, getting on a plane to Sri Lanka wouldn't look good.

I understand, and I agree, but don't you think you could miss this one protest to be at your daughter's wedding? Zoe had asked.

No, because, as we've told you all your life, you can't put individuals first. Even when they're your family.

But...

Zoe had stopped herself, because she'd long since learnt anger, discussion, spectacular gestures... Nothing pierced her parents' devotion to a plethora of causes. Zoe had tried everything and it had resulted in tragedy. Tragedy that had taught her the only way forward was to abandon all attempts to win her parents' attention, to stand on her own two feet and live the best life she could.

I know Beth will understand. Much love, darling. Bye.

Back in the present Zoe gritted her teeth—she would not let it get to her. She welcomed the knock on the door with relief, smiled as her sister entered.

'Hey,' Beth said. 'Just came to check if you were ready.' She paused and said with over-studied casualness, 'And tell you that Matt is here.'

'I'm ready.' Zoe gestured downward. 'And that's fine.' Even if her heart had chosen this moment to hammer her ribcage and she could feel nerves twist and strum inside her. At least whatever happened she looked good; one last glance in the mirror confirmed that.

Her dress was both elegant and eye-catching, a vivid bold floral mix of red and orange that would complement the red of her auburn hair. High-heeled sandals completed the ensemble, and she'd clipped her hair back with barrettes on both sides in a 'casual, but I've made an effort' style.

The whole hopefully conveyed insouciance, verve and flair and concealed the fact that inside she was a wreck.

'You sure you're OK with this?' Beth asked.

'Of course. Why wouldn't I be?' From somewhere she manufactured a light laugh. 'Matt and I were such a long time ago now— there is no reason for there to be any awkwardness.' Beth didn't know about the miscarriage—she and Matt had told no one about the pregnancy, had been waiting until the 'safe' date. The date that had never come. Then when she'd miscarried the grief and pain had been too raw and Zoe had retreated inside herself, and once her marriage had detonated, she'd run for the hills. So Beth believed that the marriage had been a foolish whim, a mistake soon realised and moved on

from without hard feelings. 'It will be good to catch up.'

Liar, liar.

But the words achieved their aim, erased the look of concern in Beth's blue eyes. 'So let's go. This is all going to be fabulous. But...I am sorry Mum and Dad aren't here.'

'Don't be. I don't think I even thought they would be. They have said they'll attend by video link so that's something. I need Mum there for some of the ceremony. Some of the rituals involve the mother-daughter relationship and she does have a role to play. At least she's agreed to do that.'

Beth and Dylan were incorporating both Sri Lankan and Western traditions in their marriage and Zoe knew they'd put a lot of thought into making it feel right, a balanced mix.

'I'm so happy how close you are to Dylan's parents.' David and Manisha had taken Beth into their family and Zoe was glad, hoped it made up for their own chaotic parents.

'Me too.' Beth grinned. 'Come on, little sis, let's go and get this party started.'

Matt Sutherland surveyed the room, forced himself not to look at the doorway, told himself to stop scanning for Zoe. It wasn't as

though he even wanted to see her; he would certainly never have solicited a meeting of his own free will. But needs must—this was Dylan and Beth's wedding—and there was no way to avoid Zoe. Especially given how small the guest list and the fact the itinerary necessitated spending masses of time together. His eyes returned to the doorway.

Perhaps it was simply a desire to get it over with, the requisite awkwardness of the initial meeting. How did one greet the woman who had turned one's life upside down, then walked out with no warning or discussion?

He'd returned home to find their penthouse flat purged of her belongings. She'd even left the windows open as if to cleanse the very air. That had oddly hurt more than anything else, the way she had so completely erased herself from their home as if showing him that she had erased him from her life.

Just as his parents had done, just as so many foster carers had done. To the latter he'd been one of many, a revolving door of troubled, traumatised, unwanted kids. Some homes he'd only been there a day or a week. But he'd nearly always arrived to a room with open windows, opened to rid the air of the child before.

But that was then and this was now. And if

he had relearnt one thing from Zoe it was to never put himself in the position of expecting loyalty or, dare he say it, love. That was how he'd survived childhood, teenage years…life. Play the game, get along, survive—but rely only on yourself, not others. That way you wouldn't get let down.

He figured he must have worked out a survival strategy from the moment he opened his eyes or perhaps even in the womb itself. His parents had been alcoholics who had pretty much ignored his existence, the first five years of his life spent in a state of criminal neglect. The only saving grace was that he couldn't actually remember it, though things would trigger panic in him even now. Hunger, or certain smells… And sometimes the nightmares still came, strange, distorted visions, faces he couldn't quite remember in the morning. Yet he'd eked out a way to survive. But his baby brother hadn't, perhaps hadn't cried loud or hard enough, had relied on a trust in his parents. Matt closed his eyes, opened them again. Now wasn't the time or the place to think about the baby brother whose life had been so brief, a brother who had fallen ill and died.

That had alerted social services and Matt had been saved. Guilt panged through him—

along with a deep yearning that he could have saved Peter.

But wishes didn't change anything; they couldn't turn the clock back. Bottom line was he hadn't. Had done nothing, couldn't even recall his brother's existence. What sort of person did that make him?

Enough. That was then, this was now.

Now he was here, on the beautiful island of Lavantivu, to celebrate his best friend's wedding. He would never forget his baby brother, but equally he had learnt to carry the memory and the guilt within him, a memory he had shared with no one—not Dylan, not Zoe, not anyone.

As if on cue his eyes roved to the doorway once again; Beth entered, and his heart lurched as Zoe came in behind her.

Any pretence of calm was a sham; it took every ounce of his iron will to keep himself still as his lungs constricted, the twisting, seething emotions becoming an uncontrollable blur. Memories filtered and streamed his consciousness in vivid images, laughter, pain, grief, anger, joy. Confusion, discomfort, failure.

Matt braced himself and focused.

He would not let Zoe back under his skin, would not give her that power.

Luckily he knew how to neutralise power—had perfected the technique in childhood. A time where he had spent so much time feeling powerless. Social workers had been in control of his life, his destiny. Their reports had influenced which foster family he would end up with and that had filled him with fear, enough so that at first he'd lashed out in panic. And so he'd been labelled as disturbed, problematic, in need of help. Matt hadn't wanted the label or the help, so he'd figured out what to do.

All he'd had to do was play the right part, be an easy placement, and so he'd submerged all his fears, anxieties, anger and confusion and he'd developed the persona they'd wanted. Well behaved, quiet but not too quiet. He'd practised a fake smile and even a fake laugh—one that sounded genuine. He'd learnt the right words to use and by doing so he'd neutralised their power. He'd been in charge.

Same with his foster families; he'd learnt how to arrive, assess the situation and the people and play his part accordingly. If they were the sort of family who preferred to treat him as a lodger he'd kept himself to himself, if they were the sort who'd wanted to believe he was 'part of the family' he'd 'muck in'. Whatever it took.

So now he would do the same, submerge

the emotion and play the part of a mature, civilised man. He would cross the room and speak to her, utter platitudes and exude non-chalance with a smile on his face. He focused on putting one foot in front of the other, aware his smile did not come as easy as usual, felt tight and forced.

Beth stepped forward to greet him first. 'Matt, thank you so much for coming. Dylan has just gone up to get his parents—they should be back any minute.'

'I wouldn't miss it for the world, and it's an amazing idea to spend a few days together.'

He turned towards Zoe—*Keep it smooth, Sutherland*—but before he could say anything a staff member approached and gestured to Beth. 'Could I speak with you, Beth?'

'Of course.' Beth turned back to Matt. 'I'll be back soon—it's probably about the lunch. I'll be right back.'

Which left him with Zoe. He turned towards her, and his rehearsed words withered and died an early death, destined to never be uttered.

She looked so familiar and yet so different.

The hair the same vibrant red hue, but longer now, falling in glossy vivid waves past her shoulders. To his own horror his fingers tingled with a need to run through the silky smoothness; he recalled doing just that. She wore heels that brought her up to his shoulder height, her head tilted up at the angle that showed off the slender column of her neck, and his gaze lingered on the spot he used to kiss. He remembered her purr of desire, the shiver that would run through her body.

Oh, hell. This had to stop. But as he met her gaze, saw the slight flush to her cheeks, the darkening of her eyes as they lingered on him, he knew she was having the same reaction. The attraction was mutual and as absolute as it had been all those years ago. But they'd learnt the hard way that attraction wasn't enough.

And still they stood rooted to the cool marble floor tiles, simply looking at each other; he needed to say something. Anything.

Seemed as if she had the same idea.

'Long time, no sex.' Her eyes widened in sheer horror, and her intake of breath spoke volumes. 'See… Long time, no *see.*'

Perhaps he should be a gentleman and go with it, pretend he hadn't heard the slip. But… 'True on both counts,' he said instead and now there was a silence, a silence fraught with tension and…and an edge, a sizzle and fizz that he truly hadn't anticipated.

And then she laughed, the gurgle of laughter he remembered, oh, so well; it lilted with sweetness and the tension dissolved and he laughed too. Then the silence returned, only this time it was spread tauter.

'So,' he said.

'So,' she said.

'So how have you been?'

'Good. Fine. How about you?'

'Good and fine as well.'

'Great.'

'Great.'

This wasn't going to go down as the world's most scintillating conversation, yet the words were meaningless. They might as well have been saying 'Blah, blah, blah'. Because the real conversation going on here was in their body language, which translated into a simmering undercurrent that he'd swear was trying to pull him towards her, encouraging him to sweep her into his arms.

This was ridiculous. Zoe had abandoned him, and, hell, he got it, even if he abhorred how she'd done it. He couldn't be the man she'd needed him to be. It had been the one part he couldn't play, couldn't pull off. But to still be attracted to her was humiliating.

'Well, now we've got that over I'll leave you to continue to circulate.' The words were foolish—as he glanced round the room he realised they were its only occupants. This was a small intimate gathering, immediate family and close friends only. Dylan's parents, Beth and Zoe's parents, Beth and Dylan and Zoe and Matt.

'That might be a bit hard,' she said.

Her gaze dropped, before flying back up to his, her cheeks flushed with embarrassment even as he said, 'Looks like we're stuck together,' and an image filled his mind of the literal meaning of the phrase. 'Until everyone else gets here,' he said hurriedly. 'Um…have your parents arrived yet?'

The question at least deflated the tension; her expression tightened. 'Unfortunately they won't be able to make it.'

For their daughter's wedding? He bit the words back, changed them to, 'That's a shame. I hope everything is all right.' During their brief ill-fated marriage he hadn't even met Zoe's parents—they had been away, had moved abroad for a six-month period, to settle in a camp of protestors who were dedicated to saving wildlife. Zoe hadn't been keen to speak about them, and when she had her words had sounded like a rehearsed spiel, a tactic he recognised because he used it himself.

Her parents were 'committed to a lifetime

of causes', 'cared deeply about the world and its many issues', had 'a lovely home in the heart of Kent', went on 'lots of protest marches' and that had been it.

And he'd respected her wish to not talk family, because he'd had no desire to discuss his background or childhood either. His spiel ran along the lines of, *My parents died when I was little; they were both only children, whose parents had died, so I had no family to go to and I ended up in care. Luckily I had good foster carers.*

'The past doesn't matter,' she'd said fiercely to him once. 'I want the present and the future to count.'

A sentiment he agreed with completely.

Only their present and future hadn't worked out. Even before the miscarriage that had precipitated Zoe's departure, their marriage had been in trouble. He'd married her, wanted to prove he would never do any wrong to his baby. How could he do any different after the way his own parents had treated him? But the sheer intimacy of it all had spooked him, the closeness made worse because for once he hadn't been able to figure out how to play the role right. The role of husband and prospective father. Because the idea of fatherhood terrified him, provoked an underlay of fear, shadowy memories that sprawled his brain and caused a pervading terror that he would be a bad parent, was genetically programmed as such.

So he'd thrown himself into work, decided to play the role of provider. Because the one thing he was definitely good at was making money. Not for nothing was he known as Midas Matt—he was a top hedge-fund manager, had been described as having an 'uncanny instinct for the markets, provided by a brilliant statistical, analytical mind'. So at least his baby would want for nothing, never feel that gnaw of hunger in his belly, have every luxury money could buy. So he'd barely seen Zoe, had escaped the emotions by avoiding their cause. And then when they'd lost the baby his emotions had escalated into a horrible churn of grief and guilt.

A black echo of how he felt about the loss of the brother he'd never known. And it had solidified a knowledge he'd had already—that it was somehow wrong for him to be a father, just as he had been unfit to be a brother.

But that had been then and this was now.

'Beth must be disappointed,' he continued.

'Of course, but it can't be helped.' Her voice was flat. 'But it does mean it's crucial that we make sure there isn't any awkwardness between us. I want this to be perfect for Beth.'

He shrugged, hoped he could carry off nonchalance even as sudden anger sparked in him. 'Awkward. Why would it be awkward?' But he could hear the edge to his voice. 'You ran out on me and our marriage. But there's no need for awkwardness—after all, you left a note. A whole paragraph.'

Two sentences, nice and easy to remember.

Dear Matt
I'm sorry to leave like this but we both know it isn't working out. The present isn't working, and I can't see a future.
Zoe

'That is not fair.' Anger blazed in her green eyes and he realised his attempt at lightness had fallen flatter than the proverbial pancake.

The hell with it. 'But it is accurate. You can't deny that.'

CHAPTER TWO

ZOE CLOSED HER EYES. It had all been going so well…or had it? The past half an hour had been a see-saw of emotion. Instant attraction—one she'd foolishly assumed had been eradicated. Foolish because their attraction had always been there, an instant, physical, chemical re-action that had only fizzled out at the very end of their marriage, subsumed by grief and confusion.

But now…hell, she'd taken one look at him, and she'd almost combusted, the shock like a lightning bolt that had still jolted her body and for a few glorious moments it had felt so good, her body alive in a way it hadn't been since their split.

Over the years she'd had a couple of brief relationships, but nothing that counted, and she'd known it wouldn't have been fair to either guy to pretend something that wasn't there.

But now anger superseded desire. How dare Matt blame her for her actions? He might be accurate in that, yes, she had left and, yes, she'd left a note, but...

'I think you may be forgetting the preceding events,' she stated. 'You had done a runner in all but name. You may have been physically present, but you had checked out of our marriage from the day I lost the baby...' Or even from the day they'd returned from their honeymoon. The words flew out as though there had been no intervening years. The past she had been running from had caught up with her and was biting her with a vengeance.

'This was a bad idea,' she said on a gasp. On all levels. She'd learnt long ago that if you were going to run, the most important thing was to not go back. She'd tried running as a child, had been the serial runaway. Back then it had been partly a bid for attention, partly a need to see if her parents truly loved her, whether they even wanted her back.

In all honesty she'd never figured out the answer. Quite often it seemed to Zoe she'd been returned, spotted by a neighbour or friend, or once by a police woman, rather than actively found by her parents.

Then, after Tom died, she'd decided the answer was to run and never look back.

His death was one Zoe felt morally responsible for—she'd taken him to the party, not knowing then how out of hand it would get. Once she'd realised there were hard drugs circulating she'd gone to find Tom, had known this was too far. She'd found him kissing another girl and she'd flipped, refused to listen or accept the excuse that he was drunk, that the girl had kissed him.

She'd stormed out. The next day she'd found out he'd accidentally overdosed, found out too that he'd been telling the truth about the girl, and the if-onlys haunted her to this day. If only she'd listened to him, forgiven him, not told him it was over, made him come with her... If only, if only, if only.

But she couldn't change history and so she'd taken her grief and guilt and tried to learn from it. Had given up her dangerous rebellious lifestyle, accepted that no amount of rebellion would attract her parents' attention, let alone their love.

And she'd run, run to university in Scotland, got a degree and after that she'd travelled, three years living out of a suitcase. Then on a trip home she'd met Matt—and life had taken on a fairy-tale quality. Somehow a first date had led to a one-night stand that had led to another date and another and they'd coasted along for months. She'd got a room and a job in London and had steadfastly refused to be carried away by his wealth or lifestyle. Had insisted on only going to places where she could pay half, and soon instead of going out they were cooking together, concocting meals, getting closer in some ways, though they never discussed the past or the future except in the most superficial terms.

Those months had felt like a bubble, a pause on her journey away from her past. But then she'd fallen pregnant, they'd got married and the bubble had slowly deflated until eventually it had collapsed along with their marriage. But he had no right to blame the way it had ended on her.

He was the one who had led her so far up the garden path she'd been embedded in a flower bed that had turned out to be illusory. She'd been smelling the roses when she should have been scenting the coffee.

Because it had turned out the man who had stepped up to fatherhood didn't actually want a child. She'd questioned whether it was that he didn't want a child with her, asked him why.

Could still remember how his expression

had closed, shadowed, and then had come the next revelation. 'I don't want to be a parent. But I do want to help children—one day I want to set up a foundation to help children in care.'

The irony had hit her with a clang. Matt was like her parents—he was a man with a cause. But clearly he recognised that meant he couldn't also be a good parent. And Zoe honoured that but knew she couldn't live with it. But how she wished he'd told the truth from the start—because otherwise she would have watched her dreams of a family fade into a repeat of her own childhood. Being put in second place for 'the greater good'.

So she'd left; maybe it had been the coward's way out, maybe she should have tried to explain, but there hadn't seemed to be a point. Bottom line was they weren't right for each other and never had been, the whole marriage an ill-fated, poorly-thought-out venture from the start.

She glared at him now; she wouldn't back down. 'Look, if I had a choice we wouldn't both be here—but there is no choice and I really do not want to make a scene and ruin Beth and Dylan's wedding.'

He inhaled deeply and rubbed his right temple in a brief, all too familiar gesture. 'Agreed. My bad. I was attempting humour and it came out wrong. As you said, we don't want any awkwardness so let's leave the past in the past. At least no one witnessed our conversation.' He glanced round, a small frown on his face. 'I wonder where they are though?'

Worry touched Zoe. 'Actually, it is a bit strange.' She was sure that leaving Zoe alone with Matt for so long had not been part of her sister's plan. She looked at her watch. 'Plus, it's supposed to be the lunch in five minutes.'

They glanced at each other. 'Come on,' Matt said. 'Let's go and see what's happening.'

They headed towards the doorway and Zoe sucked in a breath as they collided, the brush of his skin sent desire surging through her, and she was rocked back in time to delicious, incandescent memories. The simplest of touches from Matt had always been enough to ignite desire, the reaction instant and welcome. Back then.

Right now it was not welcome at all. Stepping back hurriedly, she gestured for him to go first, all too aware of her flushed face and his ability to read her body's reactions as easily as he could his own. He always had, right from that first tumultuous date. It was as if she was an open book to him and he to her, both knowing exactly what the other wanted by some basic primal instinct.

She took a deep breath in an attempt at calm and followed him, tried not to allow her gaze to linger on the breadth of his back; she'd always loved its scope, the strength of his shoulders, the assured lithe power of his walk. *Stop.* This was not helping matters at all.

But then she saw his body tense and as he quickened his step she did too and then they were both running towards the scene ahead.

Zoe gasped as she saw Dylan bent over a prone body on the floor, saw Beth in urgent conversation with a member of the catering staff, saw Dylan's mother white-faced on the sofa.

'What happened?' Zoe asked.

'It's Dylan's dad. He collapsed suddenly— we think it may be a heart attack.'

'What can I do to help?' Zoe thought quickly and then turned to the hotel staff member. 'When will the ambulance arrive?' She wasn't sure how Sri Lanka's health system worked.

'It should not be too long. Our service is relatively new but very good in this part. He will be taken to a private hospital in the city, but it is some way from here.'

'Is there anything you can do to quicken it up?'

The man thought and then his face cleared. 'I can't, but I know the hotel ten minutes away has a doctor staying; my sister works there and she served her table.'

He raced away and a minute later returned. 'She is on her way.'

True to his word, a few minutes later a petite lady raced in and moments later was stooped over David.

Beth squeezed her sister's hand. 'Thank you. Good thinking. I just can't think straight. David is…'

'I know.' And Zoe did understand. David was like a father to Beth, in truth a better one than their real dad.

'I'm so glad you're here. Both of you.' Beth nodded at Matt, who was sitting next to Manisha, had her hand in his.

Zoe nodded again—Beth had told her how much David and Manisha liked Matt. Had done ever since Matt had stepped in to protect Dylan from bullies. Dylan was dyslexic and had been small for his age. Matt had stopped the bullies in their tracks and had then taken Dylan under his wing, had encouraged him to go to the gym and learn to defend himself. Looking at Dylan now, it was hard to believe he had ever been anything other than strong, but Dylan's parents had been very grateful to Matt, and Matt in turn was fond of them.

Beth blinked back tears. 'You won't go, will you?'

Zoe's heart twisted. Beth never asked anything of her, had always been the calm one, the one who got on with things in the background. 'Of course not.'

As she spoke, Matt and Dylan came towards them.

Matt spoke quickly, his voice deep and calm. 'The ambulance is here. Dylan and his mum are going with them, but there won't be room for Beth so I've sorted out a car and a driver and Zoe and I can come with you.'

Beth nodded. 'Thank you. But…' She reached for Dylan's hand. 'There is so much to do. I'll need to cancel the wedding, sort out—'

'I'll do it,' Zoe said. 'Truly, Beth. You need to be with Dylan and the family right now. Matt can go to the hospital with you, I'll sort everything else out.'

Beth sniffed and wiped her eyes. 'Thank you. And thank you both for agreeing to stay—it means a lot to us knowing you are here.'

'It's fine.'

Zoe realised that Beth was clearly too distraught to realise that she hadn't even asked Matt to stay. But it didn't matter. This was the sister who had always been there for her, from their childhood when it had been Beth who worked out how to cook pasta, how to manoeuvre a tin opener, how to make baked beans on toast. How to coax Zoe into being a 'good girl' when they were dumped on a succession of long-suffering family friends or neighbours.

In the darkest days after Tom's death, it had been Beth's shoulder she'd cried on.

So, 'It's no problem at all. Is it, Matt?'

The slightest indication of a jaw clench, the only tell that he'd probably rather shoot himself in the foot. Otherwise his expression was the perfect blend of acquiescence.

'Of course it isn't. The priority here is David. Anything I can do to help, I will. Now let's go.'

Hours later Matt let out a sigh as he approached Zoe's villa, felt soothed by the early evening breeze with its scent of carnations that blew away the sterile antiseptic hospital smell that had seeped into his skin.

The front door was on the latch and he pushed it open, walked down the wide marble-floored hallway and into the lounge area, where Zoe was at the lacquered desk, her laptop open. She turned as he entered and rose to her feet, anxiety in her green eyes.

'It's OK,' he said. 'David is OK.'

'Beth called to say that, but she still sounded frantic.'

'It was all a bit touch-and-go at times, but he is now stable and in one of the best private hospitals in Sri Lanka. And the doctors are cautiously optimistic. There's a chance they may have to do a bypass, but the surgeon has got an amazing reputation and the fact that David looks after his health is a big plus.'

She let out a breath. 'I hope, and I believe that he will pull through. Anything else is unthinkable.' She folded her arms round her midriff and he could see the tiredness in her stance, the worry around her eyes, and suddenly an urge gripped him to reach out and put his arm around her and pull her close. An urge he knew he should shut down. 'I can't bear what losing David would do to Beth; she adores him and Manisha. They welcomed her in from the start, treated her like a daughter. He was there for Beth with advice, helped her when she was looking to retrain, gave her real support. She will be devasted if…'

She broke off and he could see the concern

in her face, wondered now about Zoe and Beth's real father, who clearly did not provide any support at all. Realised too how close the sisters were and he couldn't help but wonder what would have happened if his baby brother had survived. Would they have been close? Of course they would; he would have looked out for him, had his back. Or would he?

Guilt twisted inside him as the unanswered questions drummed his brain. Why couldn't he remember his brother? Why hadn't he tried to help him? Why had he survived and Peter hadn't? Even his brother's name was only gleaned from a conversation with a foster carer, who had assumed he knew he had a brother. The remembered shock still reverberated through his body, as his childhood self had processed the stark facts. His brother had been called Peter, had always been sickly, and had died of pneumonia aged five months. Though if he'd been treated sooner, perhaps he would have survived. If only Matt had got help; instead it had been through the intervention of a neighbour that social services had been called in.

Sadness for the past mingled with a sadness for the day's events, the threat of death that had ruined a day that should have been a happy one. Now, seeing Zoe's distress, he couldn't help himself, he did move closer, though he held his arms by his side. 'I truly think David will be OK—he is definitely in good hands. So let's focus on doing all we can do to help Beth and Dylan.'

She nodded and now a small rueful smile tipped her lips. 'Including staying here. Together.' Now the atmosphere subtly shifted, an awareness of their proximity pervading the air. 'I suppose at least we're in separate villas, so we won't be on top of each other.'

The words fell from her lips and they both froze, as the whole atmosphere changed, just like that. He knew she was replaying the same memory stream as he was, that their hormones had picked up on the words and decided to spin them into literal images.

Her cheeks flushed as she gazed at him. 'I…' She closed her eyes as though to block him out, then opened them again, gave a small shaky laugh. 'I'm sorry. I don't know why I keep opening my mouth and things like that emerge. I—'

'You do know why, Zoe.' He would not let her hide behind disingenuity; he wanted this attraction as little as she did, but he wouldn't pretend it didn't exist.

'Why?' The syllable was breathless, the chemistry so hot and vivid and alive he figured he could take a university degree in it on the spot. And somehow, right now, all the emotions, the anger, the trauma, the sadness of the past hours made it seem imperative to seize this moment and damn the consequences.

'Because all I have wanted to do since I saw you is this.'

As he stepped towards her she moved towards him; he could see the pulse pound in her throat, saw the taut neediness of her body, knew her every nerve end was tingling just as his were.

She gave a small sigh. The familiarity of her scent spun his head, and he glanced down as she laid a hand against his chest and looked up at him, her eyes wide, flecked with green glints of desire. Reaching up, she ran her fingers, oh, so gently down his jawline, the touch soft and sensuous, and he cupped her face in his hand. Her lips parted, and now he was no more capable of stopping this momentum. It would be simpler to stop breathing altogether.

One kiss—there could be no harm in that. A bittersweet reminder of the past.

Then he did kiss her, and it felt gloriously familiar and yet, oh, so new. And as she moaned a fierce satisfaction rocketed through him and he deepened the intensity of the kiss, wanted to plunder the sweetness of her lips.

She pressed against him, and his fingers tangled in the glossy silk of her hair.

Then the sound of a bird, an echoing, haunting cry, permeated the fugue of desire and they sprang apart, stood, their ragged breaths mingling as they stared at each other in mirrored horror.

What the hell was he doing? Had he no pride? This woman had left him, he hadn't seen or heard from her in four years, and now what? A few hours and he had given in to the still-present humiliating attraction.

Zoe looked as appalled as he felt. Panic widened her eyes, her cheeks were still flushed, her lips slightly swollen, her hair dishevelled. Turning, she said in a low voice, 'That shouldn't have happened. I suggest we make sure we minimise any contact at all from now on. And we erase that kiss from our memory banks.'

With that she turned and headed for the door.

'Wait.' For a moment he thought she'd ignore him, then she turned back.

'What?'

'Where are you going?'

'Anywhere but here.'

Irrational anger touched him at her need to get away from him. 'The Zoe Trewallen trademark reaction. If the going gets tough, run away.'

'Excuse me? I am not running away. I am leaving an awkward, embarrassing situation.'

He took a deep breath, knew he shouldn't let anger dominate. This was his fault and he wouldn't take it out on Zoe. 'You're right, awkward and embarrassing sums it up, but I don't think pretending it didn't happen or walking away from it will help.'

'So what do you think will help?' The question was asked with a heavy dose of sarcasm, for which he could hardly blame her.

'Well…' He paused, tried to gather his thoughts. 'I didn't expect this attraction to still exist. I thought we were over and done with and the attraction was dead.'

'Me too.'

'Well, clearly it isn't. So we have a problem. Because this will keep on happening. If the end of our marriage and four years apart hasn't doused it, we need to work out what will. We are going to keep seeing each other because of Dylan and Beth—complete avoidance isn't possible. In the next days, or hours even, they will need us. In the years to come there will be birthdays, family occasions. If they have children, they will most likely want us to be godparents. So whatever is going on here—' he gestured between them '—I'd like to kill it off now.'

'And exactly how do you propose to do that?'

It was an excellent question and one he wasn't sure he had the right answer to. 'Spend time together. Remind each other exactly why we can't work. That should have the knock-on effect of eradicating attraction as well.' In theory. 'What do you think?'

CHAPTER THREE

WHAT DID SHE THINK? In this precise moment Zoe wasn't sure she could think at all—everything seemed too overwhelming. Her lips still tingled, her head still spun from the impact of a kiss that had left her shivery with desire, frustration still churned in her gut in a seething yearning for more. Even as her common sense uttered outrage at her body's stupidity in succumbing to the lure of attraction.

Was that what Matt meant—that they needed to somehow allow common sense and sanity the upper hand, use them to quell the primal hormonal surge and the seething emotions? Because he was right. This didn't feel like a lapse of four years since the day she'd walked out. This felt as if they'd picked up right from where they'd left off. And that wasn't going to work, not as long as Dylan and Beth factored in their lives.

Plus, if she didn't get rid of this…this…

'Matt effect', then she would never meet Mr Right, would always be haunted by this man, and then how would she ever have the family she was determined to have?

So whilst all her instincts told her to run, whilst she kept her eye on the open door, she forced herself to stay still, to consider his words. Came to the reluctant conclusion he was right: running was not a viable option. As if sensing her hesitation, he continued, 'Let's go and have dinner. Have a sensible conversation to demonstrate how wrong we are for each other and that should knock attraction on the head.'

Danger! Danger! Danger! called a klaxon in her brain. Yet perhaps if she spent time with him she would recall all the excessively good reasons why she'd left. Optimism made a surge forward; perhaps over dinner she'd remember she'd built him up into something he wasn't, see that all they'd ever had was attraction and a desire to force things to work for the sake of the baby.

'OK,' she said. 'Let's do it. After all, we do need to eat.' Her stomach growled as if to underline the fact. 'I just need five minutes to freshen up.' Any more than that and she would chicken out, would run clucking over the horizon. 'Then there is a list of recommended restaurants in the kitchen—we can go to the closest.'

Ten minutes later she glanced sideways at Matt and her tummy lurched. He looked gorgeous—the shower-spiked damp hair, the lithe swell of his sun-kissed forearm that caught her breath, the jut of his jaw, the firm mouth that had wreaked havoc with her senses mere minutes before. The whole damn package.

It occurred to her that, five minutes in, the plan was *already* not working, so the quicker they got to the restaurant, the better. Yet she could hardly march there and as they walked it was impossible not to be affected by the sultry evening breeze, the scent of the flowers that mingled with the puffs of red dust from the path, the shriek of birds, the dusky cobalt blue of the sky against the sweep of the palm trees, their fronds waving gently in the breeze.

It all fuzzed her brain, as did his sheer male proximity, the tantalising scent of the shower gel that was, oh, so familiar, signature Matt—and he smelled so good—the confident stride, the way he was always so focused on the moment.

Gritting her teeth, Zoe tried to ground herself, remind herself that this was not a first date with potential—this was a closure meeting, with the view of achieving civil indifference.

'Here we are.'

'Oh.' Zoe came to a halt. This was beautiful.

Fairy lights cascaded down, twinkled in the dusky scent-laden air. The outside dining area was arranged under a thatched bamboo roof, the tables simple wooden squares surrounded by benches. Candlelight flickered on each table and the tantalising smell of spices rode the air.

Fronded palm trees fluttered over the whole edifice and flowering plants laced the roof and supporting posts in a froth of green spiky leaves and white blooms that added a fresh sweetness to the air.

A waiter approached and soon they were sitting at one of the tables, the candlelight pooling a circle of illumination that complemented the starlight that twinkled down.

She studied the menu, with both professional and personal interest, then looked up to see Matt watching her.

'What are you going to have?' she asked, knowing how much he enjoyed his food. It was something they had in common—food was an important part of their lives. For Zoe it was because she'd never been sure where the next meal would come from. Her parents would get distracted sometimes and simply assumed Zoe and Beth would learn to fend for themselves. After all, 'You need to realise how lucky you are, darlings, living here with so much to eat.'

And Zoe understood that, she really did, but it did seem that sometimes their parents didn't realise that the plentiful food supplies were in the shops and Zoe and Beth were unable to access them. Or if there were supplies it wasn't always easy to work out exactly how to cook them.

Zoe had tried to get these points across, yelled and screamed when simple discussion hadn't prevailed, but she hadn't been able to permeate her parents' dense shield of protection. Sometimes she wondered if they simply didn't see her or had some sort of filter that retranslated her words and actions. Beth had taken a different route, accepted her parents would never change and had worked out how to cook pasta, how to access what there was.

But to Zoe that had been giving in. She'd wanted her mum to cook her dinner, to have family meals, wanted to have friends round and have a mum or dad who made sausages and mash, and then took them to the park for ice cream.

But, sweetheart, there are so many more important things to do. Maybe your friends could help us leaflet drop.

She shook off the thoughts, reminded herself that she too had accepted that her parents would never change. But one day, when she had kids, they would have proper home-cooked meals, and she would never miss a single sports day or school concert. And she would listen to them and…

'You OK, Zoe?'

'Yes. Sorry.' She turned her attention back to the menu. 'I was thinking of asking if they would do a taster plate so I can sample everything—that way…'

'It takes away the need to choose,' he said with a sudden smile.

And for a minute she was transported back in time to the halcyon weeks they'd spent together when they weren't married, she wasn't pregnant, and they'd just been happy. They'd visited a restaurant from a different country every week, bought cookbooks, experimented with recipes. Hand in hand, talking about food and spices, arguing over the merits of paprika and cayenne—what had happened to them?

His face softened as if he too was revisiting happy memories.

Once they'd ordered he leant back, picked

up his bottle of beer and took a sip. 'So, Dylan told me you've spent the past years working your way round the world.'

'Maybe not the world, but as much of it as I can. I wanted to learn as much as I could about cooking in different countries—I've got a plan.' At first all she'd wanted was to run, to get away from the sadness and the grief and the sense of betrayal and stupidity. So she'd done literally that, run away, started travelling again, but this time she'd decided to instil her travel with a purpose. Because after the miscarriage she'd known that, no matter what, she wanted a family. And in order to have that she needed security, a job, a career.

'Tell me.'

She hesitated and he smiled. 'I'm really interested.'

'I want to open a restaurant and I want it to offer cuisine from round the world. I would either do theme nights, or theme months. So a country a night or a month.'

'It sounds a bit like what we used to do,' he said. 'When we picked a country every week and chose a recipe to cook.' His words arrested her; she hadn't even realised that fact, but he was right, and she wasn't sure how that made her feel. As if he sensed her ambiguity, he gestured. 'Anyway, go on.'

'So I've spent the last few years working my way around different restaurants—I've tried to do different roles so I understand the business side of it as well as the actual cooking. I've had in-depth discussions with accountants, chefs, managers, waiting staff… everyone. I've just finished a contract, covering maternity leave in a restaurant in Switzerland, and after Sri Lanka my plan is to return to the UK and get started. I'll give myself a year or so to get up and running and then I can get on with the next part of the plan.'

'Which is?'

'I want a family, to settle down. I want to have children and I don't want to leave it too late.' She met his gaze full on, realised she was holding her breath. Ridiculous. What was she hoping? That he'd say, *What a good idea. By coincidence, me too. I've changed my mind and become a family guy.*

'So you're in a relationship?'

Had she imagined it or had his body tensed as he'd asked the question? Was there a fleeting clench of his jaw?

Before she could respond the waiter approached with their food.

Matt focused on the ensuing conversation, entered into the discussion on 'turmeric, lime leaves…wine should complement it, but so would tea…vanilla pods, cardamom…' with an enthusiasm aimed to deflect the sense of edginess inspired by the idea that Zoe had found someone to settle down with.

He should, he knew, be pleased if she had, or at least indifferent, but… No buts. No way would he acknowledge even a tremor of jealousy. What was wrong with him? Envy or jealousy were not his style—he'd realised long ago there was no point. When he'd seen families that worked, parents who looked after and cared for their kids, who hugged them, *loved* them, of course he'd been jealous until he'd figured out jealousy changed nothing. It couldn't give him a different past— the facts were his parents hadn't looked after him, or cared, and hadn't loved him. Had seen nothing in him worthy of love. That was the truth and no amount of jealousy could alter that fact. The emotion did nothing but cause him pain. In truth, he'd come to that conclusion about most emotions, and so he'd learnt to cut them off. Just as he would now.

And so he would not show undue curiosity, or allow even a tinge of negative emotion, and when the waiter finally departed, he gestured to the food. 'You go first.' Waited as

Zoe helped herself to some of the aromatic curry, tore off a piece of *roti* and dipped it in.

'This is incredible,' she said. 'Try it. I think it's the *kukul mas* curry, which is chicken curry but not as we know it.'

He took a spoonful and tasted it and for a second was genuinely diverted from thoughts of Zoe's relationship status. 'Fennel seeds. Coconut milk.'

'Definitely. And *pandan* leaves. I came across them in Thai cooking as well. They are long spiky leaves and you can use them to wrap food in before cooking it. Or you boil them up for the juice and add them to curries.'

He waited a few more minutes whilst they both sampled the *wambatu moju*, a delicious aubergine pickle, and the *gotu kola sambol*, a salad made from a shredded green vegetable, pennywort, combined with chillies, shallots and freshly grated coconut.

Then, finally, with exactly the right degree of nonchalance, he said, 'So where were we? Oh, yes. You're planning on settling down. Does that mean you're in a relationship?'

'No!' She put down her piece of coconut *roti* and stared at him. 'Obviously I wouldn't have kissed you if I was with someone. So, no, I'm not in a relationship yet but I'm working on it.'

'How?' The edginess increased. Was she out there dating a variety of men? Was she using dating apps? Why the hell did he even care? The dog-in-the-manger attitude was not one he was comfortable with. This was all about getting rid of the attraction between them and making sure they could move on without baggage. So the fact she had a plan to settle down was a good thing—made it crystal clear that any lingering attraction was pointless.

'It's a work in progress. I've devised a system—I just haven't tested it out yet.'

Relief tempered the unease and now curiosity surfaced. 'What sort of system?'

'Well, in the past few years I've dated a couple of guys…but they didn't work out. One of them was a great guy, we got on, we had shared interests…blah, blah, blah. But there was no spark at all and I didn't think that was fair.'

'And the other one?' Guilt twinged inside him that he was happy to hear about these strangers' shortcomings.

'He was too…serious. I couldn't imagine falling about laughing with him and that kind of ruined it. Sometimes I wanted to have a frivolous conversation about silly things. So I guess there was no real spark there either.'

It occurred to him that miraculously he and Zoe had managed to laugh earlier that day—despite the anger and the awkwardness, they had still managed to laugh.

'So the system doesn't seem to be working.'

She shook her head. 'No, they were why I devised a system. I realised the "seems like a good guy…let's see what happens" approach wasn't working. So now I have put together a tick list, a questionnaire. So the deal-breaker is whether or not he wants a family. If not, that's it—we go no further. If he does, I work out his test score in the remaining areas, analyse the data. If they tick enough boxes, I'll try a second date.'

'Assuming anyone wants a second date. I've spotted the flaw. Don't you feel the questionnaire may be a little off-putting?' he pointed out.

She grinned at him. 'Ha-ha! I'm not going to actually sit there with a pen and paper or hand them a questionnaire. It'll be more *subtle* than that.'

Raising his eyebrows, he gestured with one hand. 'Give me an example.'

She tilted her head to one side as she considered. 'OK. For example, if I need to know if we share a sense of humour, I'll tell a joke or a funny story and see if he gets it or not.'

'Let me guess—you've already compiled a list.'

'How did you know that?'

'Because I know you. I remember the spreadsheets and lists and research you used to do. Go on, try me with a joke and I'll tell you if it sounds natural.'

'OK. So let's say we're chatting about work and you've told me what you do. So you tell me you're an investment manager, or that you own an investment company. Then I say how interesting that is, ask a couple of intelligent questions to ascertain your ethics and then I go, "Hey, I've got a joke you may like. Why is a skateboard a good investment?"'

Matt stared at her. He knew he should focus on the answer, but he couldn't. Her expression was animated in the candlelight, her green eyes bright, her lips upturned as she waited for him to reply. Damn it. All he wanted to do was kiss her. Instead he was helping her prep for a first date.

'Do you give up?' she asked.

'I give up. Why is a skateboard a good investment?'

'Because you can flip it.' Her smile widened into a grin and the sheer absurdity brought an answering smile to his face, followed by a chuckle.

'That is a terrible joke,' he said when the laughter subsided.

'I know, right? But it is still funny.'

'I don't think you can slate a guy for not having a sense of humour if he doesn't laugh at that quality of joke.'

'You laughed…' There was a silence and something shimmered in the air. Hurriedly he helped himself to another helping of *dal* and rice.

'Which proves my point. Because I am definitely not the kind of guy you're looking for. But I get that a sense of humour is important. What else will you be vetting for?'

'Spark,' she said, and the very word seemed to alight the connection.

'So how do you figure out if there's a spark or not?' He could hear the tightness in his voice, her gulp audible before she replied.

'I thought I'd orchestrate an accidental brush of our hands.' She picked up one of the small bowls and held it out. 'Like this.'

He held his hand out over the candle, knew he was literally playing with fire, and took one of the fritters and as he did so allowed his hand to brush against hers. The lightest of contacts yet it sent a fierce jolt through him.

'Then,' she continued, her eyes wide now, 'I could offer to read their fortune. Tell them I'm interested in palmistry.'

Now he held his hand out palm up and she took it in hers. Jeez, his whole body tautened as she, oh, so slowly ran a finger over his hand, along the grooves and lines. He heard her breath catch in her throat and desire rocked through him at the sound, at the sensation of her touch.

'I...' She blinked and dropped his hand. 'I'm sorry. That was not supposed to happen.'

'Or at least not with me,' he said.

'No.' She sat back, picked up her water glass and gulped, then took a sip of wine. 'Definitely not with you. But actually I don't want that to happen with anyone. It's too much. I want a tingle. A *faint* tingle.'

'Why? I thought you were looking for spark.'

'Spark, not forest fire. Attraction is important but it's not the be-all and end-all. Too much attraction complicates things, masks other flaws. We're proof of that.'

Maybe she was right. Attraction had caught them up in a vortex and propelled them into a pregnancy, a marriage, a disaster.

'It also distracts from problems because you solve them with sex. That's what we did.

And when we didn't have that any more it turned out we didn't have anything. We were so blinded by attraction we didn't really get to know each other. I won't risk that again. Because the most important thing for me, the deal-breaker, is whether he wants a family. He needs to be decent and hard-working, willing to put his family first, be a hands-on dad and be able to give our children love and fun and attention and support.'

Her voice was fervent and Matt suddenly realised how very far short he had fallen from what she wanted and needed. He was decent and hard-working, but the ticks stopped there. The rest of it was out of his zone of experience. The idea of being hands-on brought him out in a clammy sweat—what if he got it wrong? What if he hurt his own child, or messed up in some way? The best he could have done, would have done if they hadn't lost the baby, was provide—his child would never have gone hungry, never wanted for anything money could buy.

But that life path had closed and couldn't be reopened, and he understood exactly why Zoe was looking for a Mr Right so different from him. Yet...

'That all sounds grand, but what about you?'

'What do you mean?'

'Surely he needs to be a good husband as well, be there for you when you need him.' Guilt suddenly twinged inside him in the knowledge that he hadn't been there for her, in her grief. His own grief, so intense, the echo of the loss of his baby brother, the fear that somehow it was all his fault, that he should have looked after Zoe better, had somehow rendered him unable to do anything. The harder he'd tried to do the right thing, the more he hadn't been able to because the one thing she'd wanted to make it better he couldn't give her—the promise of a family.

But his flaws didn't mean she should settle. 'I get your Mr Right has to be proper dad material, but he has to be right for you on a personal level as well.'

'Of course, and any decent man with a sense of humour who loves his kids will be right for me.'

'But he needs to care…to love you too.' The idea didn't sit well with him. If he was honest his prime desire right now was to take the mythical Mr Right and shake him by the scruff of his neck before hurling him superhero-style up to a planet far, far away. But that wasn't the point.

'I don't think that matters; I'm not looking

for grand romantic love. I don't want us to be so wrapped up in each other that our kids lose out. They need to come first.' The certainty in her voice was absolute. 'I want to be a happy family. I think that means I need to have a partner who has the same outlook on family.'

'I understand that. But your relationship is important as well—after all, once the children have left and as they grow up it is that man who you will spend your life with. That's the man you'll wake up to every day.'

Memories filtered through again, of waking up with Zoe in the crook of his arm, warm and secure, tendrils of her soft red hair tickling his chest. And then other memories, of the last few weeks when his nightmares had returned and he'd slip from the room, not wanting to disturb her, or even admit to having those night terrors he'd thought he'd licked in childhood.

Yet another reason why he wasn't programmed for family life.

'I understand that, and I know what I'm doing.'

'So what happens if you can't find a Mr Right? Will you settle for Mr Nearly Right? Or Mr I Only Tick One Box or—'

'If I can't find a man I want to settle down with, a man I believe will provide a happy family life, then I will become a single mother. Simple.'

'Is it that simple?'

'It is still possible to use a donor, but it is much more complicated now legally. So perhaps I would ask a friend or perhaps I would adopt. But, one way or another, I know I want to be a mum. I'd way prefer my child to have a hands-on dad, but if that's truly not possible I won't give up being a parent.'

He saw the fervour in her eyes, could see how important a family was to her, and guilt pierced him once again that he'd let her down so badly. Guilt and a renewed sadness that they'd lost the baby—what would have happened if their child had been born? Would he have managed to be the hands-on dad she wanted? Would he have been able to love the baby as he presumably hadn't loved his brother? Or would he have felt nothing? Would he have spent years faking emotion? The questions all unanswerable. Pointless.

'I truly hope you achieve your dreams,' he said softly. 'However you do it.' The one thing for sure, he wouldn't be part of them. So there was little point allowing emotions to the table. Time to change tack, however abruptly.

'So now how about we get dessert?' he suggested.

'Good idea,' she said. 'We've talked about me, so once we've ordered we can talk about you.'

Marvellous.

CHAPTER FOUR

ZOE WAITED UNTIL the waiter had deposited the *halapa* in front of them, explained that the dessert was made from a *kanda* leaf filled with honey, flour and sugar mixture.

'You will definitely want another one.'

'I am sure we will.' A sentiment she knew was correct as she bit into the tangy green concoction.

Placing the parcel down, she then looked across at Matt, his dark eyes slightly wary, his six o'clock shadow more pronounced, and somehow the prospect of her Mr Right seemed to fuzz around the edges.

No!

That was attraction speaking and exactly why spark was so dangerous and unwanted.

'So, your turn,' she said. 'Tell me what you've been doing the past four years. Moving towards domination of the financial world?' she quipped, trying to keep her voice light, to not rekindle the confusion and resentment she'd felt about his work. She'd loved that he loved his job, but she'd hated the hours he devoted to it, the ever-increasing time away from her.

He'd told her he was doing it 'for the baby'. But she hadn't got it; when she'd met him he was already an uber-successful hedge-fund manager, he'd worked for a prestigious investment company, owned a swish London apartment, had a fridge stocked with food and drink, luxurious furniture, an expensive car. He hadn't flaunted any of it, had seemed content with simple ownership, but he surely hadn't needed to work even harder.

But he'd claimed he did. Had wanted to set up his own business. 'That way I'll be in control. It'll be down to me how well we live and how much security I can provide.'

Which begged the question: How much security did any one family need?

'But we can budget, economise. Plus, I'll be earning as well and I don't need luxury.' Then she'd seen the set of his lips and had wondered if maybe he did.

'I know that. But I want my child to have the best I can give him.'

'But…' She'd trailed off. 'The best you can give him is yourself.'

He'd glanced away and then back at her. 'Sure, I get that.'

But he hadn't. In actual fact, it turned out that Matt had quite simply never wanted the baby, didn't want a family, had only married Zoe as a matter of honour and principle. The idea still sent a sheen of humiliation over her, along with a knowledge that his work ethic had simply been a means of escaping her, the reminder of the responsibility he hadn't wanted. Yet it seemed that he had done what he had wanted to do—

'Beth told me you've set up by yourself.'

'I have. I set up Sutherland Investments two years ago.'

'And you're doing pretty well.' Before coming to Sri Lanka she'd done what she hadn't done for four years—an Internet search on Matt—and discovered exactly how well he was doing. His investment company had won coveted business awards and, whilst small and niche, it was exclusive and had a more than enviable track record.

'Yes. I've got a growing client base. I've taken on a few employees, including an excellent second in command. So I can juggle my time however I want.'

'So you get more free time? To do what? Race fast cars, spend time on a luxury yacht?'

Somehow that was hard to picture. It was something she'd never worked out about Matt—he owned the requisite trappings of wealth, but she was pretty sure he didn't need them. She wasn't even sure he liked them—he'd barely driven the fast car in his garage, didn't seem to pay a lot of attention to shopping, though all his clothes were super expensive.

'No. I do have a couple of flash cars and a fancy apartment, but most of my spare time and money is spent on my foundation. The one I told you about.'

'That's great.' She could hear the flatness in her voice and the guardedness in his, loathed herself for it.

But she couldn't help it. The echo of her parents jarred on her. The knowledge Matt had decided to prioritise a cause over a family still…hurt.

'Tell me about it,' she said now, knowing this was the best way to kill attraction stone-cold dead.

He shook his head. 'It's OK. I can be very boring when I get on my hobby horse.'

'That's a good thing. We're reminding each other why we're bad for each other, remember? So the more tedious, the better.' Only somehow she suspected Matt couldn't be tedious however hard he tried.

She watched as he marshalled his thoughts, the slight crease to his brow, the intensity in his dark eyes. 'I started out with simple donations, but since my company took off I've been able to do more. I knew it was bad, but I hadn't realised how widespread the problem is. So many kids in care, so many youngsters caught up in a life where crime seems to be the only option, so many without a family to look out for them and care for them. Some of them trapped in families who patently don't care for them. My foundation aims to help as many as possible.'

It was a fervour she recognised all too well, the clarion call of a man who had a cause. She understood too that Matt had a reason for his fervour; he himself had been in care, though he had hardly ever spoken about it. Only to say that he had been one of the lucky ones who'd had good carers who had provided all he'd needed.

'We do a lot of different things, from organising food banks to a programme of activities, career advice, private tuition at centres throughout the UK. We also offer counselling and therapy. I've got great dedicated managers and I try to be as hands-on as possible as well.'

'That sounds incredible.' And it did. 'And like a second job.'

'Yes, it is—it all certainly keeps me busy. But it's fun as well, and really rewarding. Some of the kids blow my mind.'

Zoe frowned, realised she'd never heard her parents call what they did fun or rewarding—to them it was a mission, a road strewn with obstacles. 'It must be frustrating sometimes too.'

'Sure, but whilst I realise whatever I do there's more to be done, I have to believe I am making a difference.'

'It sounds like what you do makes an enormous difference.' And it did, yet she knew her voice still lacked the enthusiasm he deserved, and Matt had noticed; she could see from his face that he was perplexed, and she ploughed on hurriedly. 'What about relationships? How do you find the time?'

'I don't. As we both figured out, I am not relationship material; to be honest, I don't want to be. My life works how it is now. I've got the right balance. I'm not planning a life of celibacy, but I am happy with short-term and uncomplicated. The type of relationship where you kick back and relax for a while, have fun in and out of bed, and then resume normal life.'

'So a bit like recharging your batteries?' She knew she sounded snarky, but somehow she couldn't help it.

'Exactly and what's wrong with that?'

'Don't you think it's a bit shallow?'

'No, I don't. And even if it is, what's wrong with shallow? In this part of my life shallow is exactly what I want if it means avoiding getting out of my depth.'

'Or you could learn to swim?'

'I tried that, Zoe. With you and it didn't work.'

He was right, but he'd only tried it because he'd felt he had to; perhaps it would be different if it was the right woman. 'Perhaps your Ms Right will come along and change your mind.'

'I'm not on the market for a Ms Right.'

'Unless she is Ms Shallow,' Zoe said, and then shook her head. 'Sorry. That's not fair.'

'No, it's not,' he agreed. 'Or not if you mean it as an insult. There's nothing wrong with paddling in the shallows—not everyone wants to swim in the deep end. I'm always honest with my partners and I do my best to make sure they are being honest with me. It works.' He gave a sudden smile. 'The shallow end can be a whole lot of fun.'

The smile sent a shiver through her; she knew he spoke nothing more than absolute truth, knew just how much fun Matt could be. But that wasn't enough—not for her. So…

'I guess we really do know now that this attraction has nowhere to go. You want shallow relationships and no family. I want Mr Right and children. That really is a never the twain shall meet. So let's hope attraction gets the picture and fades away. We have both moved on.'

'Exactly,' he said. 'I'll drink to that.'

Yet somehow the brightness of their voices sounded forced and once they had clinked bottles a silence weighted with awkwardness descended.

It was almost a relief when her phone rang. 'It's Beth,' she said, and relief morphed to anxiety. *Please let David be all right.*

Matt watched, as Zoe's face relaxed and she did a thumbs up to let him know it was OK, or at least not the worst news. She listened for a while and her expression lightened and a small smile touched her lips as she nodded.

'I think that's a wonderful idea and I'll sort it all out.' More words from Beth, and Zoe shook her head. 'I don't mind at all. Leave it all to me, and you and Dylan focus on being with David.'

She disconnected and looked across at him. 'David is OK, but they are doing the bypass surgery the day after tomorrow. Just in case anything goes wrong Beth and Dylan want to get married before the operation, so I am going to organise a hospital wedding for the morning of the op.'

'*We* are going to organise a hospital wedding.' The words fell from his lips without thought. 'Dylan is my best friend—I want to be part of trying to make this as good as it can be in the circumstances. Plus, it makes sense—it's a lot to organise in a day. It will be easier.' He raised his eyebrows. 'Why the look of surprise?'

She shrugged. 'As you're a non-believer in deep and meaningful relationships, I didn't think you'd want to organise a wedding.'

'I believe in them for other people—just not for me. I truly want to help make this as special and precious as we can. For Dylan and Beth and Dylan's parents.'

'Then I guess we should get back to the resort and come up with a plan of action.' She hesitated. 'As long as it won't be awkward.'

'Absolutely not,' he stated. 'Project wedding will keep us focused and busy—there won't be time to be awkward.'

The theory was sound, he assured himself as they started the walk back to the resort. 'So how do we go about organising a wedding in a hospital in Sri Lanka?'

'Well, Beth has discovered that it is definitely possible to do. Lavantivu has various laws surrounding "overseas weddings" and it is allowed, but there is paperwork that needs to be done.'

'I'll get on to that. I spent time in the hospital so I spoke to people there already.'

'Perfect. I'll contact the celebrant who was going to officiate if the wedding had gone ahead next week as planned. She sounded lovely—I really hope she'll be able to carry out the ceremony here. I know Beth and Dylan had in-depth conversations with her as to how they wanted it to be.' She thought for a minute. 'I'll need to call my parents to make sure they can still attend by video; Mum in particular has a part to play. Oh, and we'll need to go shopping for clothes.'

Matt slowed down. 'Clothes?'

'Beth and I were going to go and find her a dress here. She didn't want the hassle of bringing a dress over here, so we were going to make a day of it, have lunch, go to a spa and shop. Dylan and his dad and you the same.' She glanced at him. 'I take it he didn't mention it.'

'Nope. He was probably going to surprise me.'

She grinned. 'You mean he didn't want to give you a chance to wriggle out of it.'

'Something like that. But that's OK—add shopping to the list.'

They approached the garden of the villa and she paused. 'Good idea—I will make an actual list. I've got pen and paper here.' She perched on the wall that bordered the lushness of the garden and began to write and his breath hitched. Silhouetted in the starlight, Zoe looked almost ethereally beautiful. The moonbeams illuminated and highlighted the red of her hair, which rippled in the gentle balm of the breeze, emphasised the length of her eyelashes, the sweep of her cheekbones.

And it seemed as though dinner had cleared the air, and the idea of a shared goal had allowed them to walk back together, bouncing ideas off each other with no sense of awkwardness. Could it be that simple to sort out the past? Doubt touched him—they hadn't discussed the past at all—but that was OK. Why revisit pain and angst, why rake up hurt, or regurgitate arguments and mistakes?

Much better to focus on the here and now and the wedding.

She looked up and smiled and now his heart beat a little bit faster. 'So we have a plan.'

'We do.'

Perhaps she saw something in his eyes, but now everything seemed to hush, to maze around them into a haze of sweet-smelling aromas, the gentle caw of a nightbird and himself and Zoe in a timeless moment.

'I'm…glad we're doing this together,' she said softly.

'Me too.' The words sounded strangled as she rose, stepped towards him and, oh, so gently kissed his cheek, the brush of her lips sending a bittersweet thrill of desire through him along with a sense of warmth. She stood back and he could see it in her eyes, the same yearning to close the gap and this time share a different sort of kiss. He forced his feet to adhere to the ground, reminded himself that they must not succumb to attraction. Because they knew it could get them nowhere.

'Goodnight,' she said, her voice breathless, infused with panic, before she turned and left.

Matt opened his eyes, heard the sound of birds drifting in on the balmy breeze, smelt the tang of coffee in the air mixed with a heady smell of warmth and sunshine. He swung his legs out of bed, stretched and headed for the welcome cool of the shower, emerging from his villa fifteen minutes later to find Zoe sitting in the shaded garden area outside the building that housed the kitchen and eating area.

'Good morning.' Her voice was brisk and she couldn't quite meet his eye. 'I thought we could call the hospital and the celebrant and then eat. The caterers have left an amazing breakfast inside for us.'

'Sounds like a plan,' he replied, careful to keep his voice as businesslike as hers. Her hair was held up in a messy bun, she was dressed in simple, flowing, wide-bottomed trousers and a sleeveless top, her face make-up-free, and she *still* looked beautiful.

He sat down and quickly pulled out his phone to call the hospital, saw that she was doing likewise.

Ten minutes later, he hung up, just as she said, 'Thank you, we'll see you then.' He raised his eyebrows in question. 'We decided it was best for Edwina to come here to discuss the arrangements. Obviously she's already met with Beth and Dylan but we need to discuss how it will work in the hospital.' She gestured to his phone. 'What did they say?'

'It will all be OK. Beth and Dylan have already done all the paperwork allowing foreign nationals to get married here. They've presented their passports, birth certificates and certified certificates to show they are both single. The hospital would like to see the copies. David's consultant will also provide a letter confirming David is unable to leave the hospital, and that means I can get the necessary letter of permission.'

'Perfect. Now let's eat. It's going to be a busy day and I'm not going anywhere with you if you're hungry.'

'Why not?'

'Because I know you get grumpy when you don't eat.'

He blinked. 'How do you know…?' He stopped, annoyed with himself for the giveaway admission. Zoe was dead right, but he truly hadn't registered that she knew. Thought he'd long since learnt to master or at least hide his reaction to hunger. As a child, once he'd been taken from his parents his relationship with food had been problematic.

Piecing together his early years, he now knew food had been something he'd had to scavenge, probably from bins, and any person he could appeal to. With hindsight he understood that to his five-year-old's mind the sudden availability of food must have blown every nerve cell. The whole thing had sent him into a tailspin, unable to work out whether to eat the food, hide the food or assume it was some sort of trick.

A social worker had once explained to a foster carer, 'It is vitally important to keep him regulated with food. Without it he goes almost feral. His mood dips and he turns angry.'

He'd been too young to fully understand the words, but as he'd grown older he'd learnt to regulate himself, learnt that hunger triggered panic so it was best to make sure he stayed fed. That he controlled food and never let food control him.

Now Zoe looked at him in puzzlement. 'I don't know how I know. I just always thought you got a bit edgy when we'd skipped a meal.' She dipped her head to one side and contemplated him. 'Your jaw clenches. You rock back on your heels.' She gurgled with laughter. *Call me Holmes...Zoe Holmes.* 'Because I'm right, aren't I?'

He shrugged and she frowned.

'Hey, I didn't mean to upset you. Lots of people get irritable when their blood sugar levels drop. I do. Maybe that's why I recognise the signs in you.'

'It's fine. No big deal.' And it wasn't, but he loathed that his first years still had an impact on him. All he wanted was to erase them, wipe them out. Ironic the one thing he did want to remember, he couldn't—his brother. 'Let's get breakfast.'

'They've set it up inside—it is amazing. Truly. I'll take you through everything— one of the caterers explained it all and I took notes.'

He followed Zoe inside and his eyes widened at the array of food. 'Wow.'

'I know, right? So these here are hoppers. These ones are called string hoppers and they are rice noodles, pressed into flat spirals, or you can have egg hoppers. Look.' She glanced at him. 'I don't mean look at me, I mean look at the food.'

But he couldn't help it. Her face was so animated, so pretty, so full of enthusiasm it was hard not to look at her. 'Sorry. It's just… good to see you happy.' There was a silence and then he turned to the table. 'Anyway, tell me about egg hoppers.'

'Right. So instead of making noodles you fry the batter into a pancake and then you put an egg in the middle. Then you garnish it with chillies, onions and lemon juice.' She paused for breath. 'Then over here you have a kind of porridge-like dish. It's called *kiribath* and it's made of coconut milk, rice and bananas.'

'Well, it all looks incredible.' There were other dishes, as well as bowls of fruit, and *roti*, *dal* and pots of chutneys and pickles.

She piled her plate high as he did the same and they went to sit back outside.

'So what else did the hospital say?' she asked.

'They were great; we can use a room overlooking the garden so it can look pretty, and we can take photos out there after the ceremony. They are happy for us to take in flowers and decorate the room however we like.'

'Perfect.' She glanced up and, following her gaze, he saw a grey-haired woman approach. Slim and svelte, she smiled as she approached. A woman with dark brown eyes that spoke of an inner peace.

'Good morning. I'm Edwina Storrington, the celebrant. Apologies, I am here early. Please finish your breakfast.'

'Or why don't you join us?' Zoe offered. 'There is plenty inside.'

'That is most kind.' A few minutes later she sat down opposite them. 'Thank you so much for agreeing to meet with me. I thought it would be easier to sort out the details in person. First, though, is there any flexibility on the time of the wedding? I do have a prior commitment that day. I work with the local orphanage, and I have plans to take the kids out that day. These kids are let down time and again—I prefer not to add to that burden.'

'Because of the operation I don't think we can change the date.' Zoe's face fell. 'But we could do the ceremony as early as you like?'

'If the hospital can accommodate an early morning ceremony, then I should still be able to zoom off to get the minibus, to collect the kids.'

'That would work fine,' Matt said.

Edwina nodded. 'Then I am happy to go ahead. Beth, Dylan and I spoke at length about the ceremony and how they wish to have a mix of Sri Lankan and Western traditions. Can we just go through the details and see how to accommodate everything in a shorter ceremony in a hospital?'

Matt sat back and watched the two women discuss the details, free now to admire Zoe, the way she gestured with her hands, the way she gave one hundred per cent to the conversation, the gurgle of her laugh, the charm of her smile. And how much she cared about getting this right for Beth. Twenty minutes later Edwina pushed her cup away and smiled.

'I think we've covered everything. Thank you both very much for the breakfast.'

'Would it help if we pack up the rest of the food and drop it to the orphanage?' Matt offered.

Edwina smiled. 'That would be marvellous. But no need for you to drop it. I can take it there now. I pop in whenever I can anyway.'

Zoe rose. 'I'll get started. I'll go and see if I can rustle up some Tupperware.'

'Tell me about the orphanage,' Matt asked Edwina.

'It's a residential place I helped set up a few years ago. It houses up to fifteen kids up to the age of eighteen at any one time. Their backgrounds vary. There are some pretty sad stories there, yet they really all are great kids—I do my best for them and we raise as much money as we can, but it's tough. So every little bit helps.'

'So what have you got planned for them?'

'It's not a lot—I'm taking them on a picnic and they'll have a chance to run off some steam and have some fun.'

Zoe returned as they continued to speak and soon they were all packing away the food. But Matt sensed that Zoe's mood had changed, her previous enthusiasm and exuberance muted; she seemed to have distanced herself from the conversation and he wondered why. Continued to wonder as he walked Edwina to her car.

CHAPTER FIVE

ZOE WATCHED MATT walk away with Edwina, could tell their conversation was an important one by the way Matt bent his head towards the older woman, the way he moved his hands as he talked, the nod and bob of his head… She just knew. Knew too that the orphanage had sparked his interest, and to her own shame a sense of dread weighted her stomach.

She knew what would happen next: Matt would abandon their plans to shop in favour of a visit to the orphanage. She knew too that helping orphans was of course more important than shopping, and she could easily shop on her own. Knew it was not on a par with her parents' behaviour and yet…yet anger still roiled inside her. An anger she knew she had to hide, an anger she disliked herself for.

As he approached the table he looked down at her with a slightly puzzled look on his face.

'Is everything OK?'

'Of course.'

'Good. Then are you ready to go?'

Huh?

Now his frown deepened. 'We've got shopping to do, or have I missed something?'

Oh.

Perhaps she'd overreacted and she was aware of a small smile on her face as she stood up. Told herself it shouldn't matter, but it did and, like it or not, she was glad that Matt was coming shopping. Was glad that he hadn't acted as her parents would have.

'Let me grab my stuff and we'll go. I thought we'd do the dress first. I've done some research and I think I've found an ideal shop.'

'Sure. I've hired a car and a driver. That way we don't need to work out parking or worry about directions.'

'Great.'

Once in the car she turned to him. 'I really want to make this perfect for everyone.'

He nodded. 'I know you do, and I really think you will.'

'Beth told me that they are doing this as an affirmation of life, of hope and joy and to give David a sense of happiness before his operation.'

He nodded. 'I spoke with Dylan yesterday. They told David that and he said he appreciated that, but he *knows* he may not survive and he wants to see them married before the operation. David is a realist—and a statistician. He'll know there is a chance he won't make it, but that will make it even more important to him that he sees Dylan get married. If it were me, even if I were terrified, or knew my chances were low, I'd want to see my son happy, to know I'd seen him married and, yes, I'd want it to be a proper celebration, not muted by thoughts of my death.'

The words caught her and she couldn't help it—his discussion of a hypothetical son when he'd decided so categorically not to have children. Decided to put his foundation and his work first and prioritise those. A niggle touched her—Matt wasn't a man who didn't believe he could do it all. Yet he'd decided he wouldn't have children of his own.

Enough—it was no longer her business, and she was relieved when the car glided to a halt outside a row of shops.

Five minutes later they entered the welcome air-conditioned temperature. She glanced round and her eyes widened at the sheer extent of choice. The clothes on display were truly amazing, an exotic burst of colour and style…dresses, saris, cashmere shawls all draped over tables in an array that made her eye dart from piece to piece.

A smiling assistant came forward, introduced herself as Anesha, and Zoe explained what they were looking for. 'I am hoping to find something celebratory that somehow combines Sri Lankan and Western tradition and is something my sister would love.'

'I understand,' Anesha said. 'Sri Lankan brides often wear a wedding sari, known as a Kandyan sari.'

'I think Beth would feel that wasn't quite the right thing to do as she isn't actually Sri Lankan and doesn't live here.'

'Then how about a sari? Not a wedding one, but a beautiful one none the less.'

'I think Beth and Manisha would like that, and, as it is a small wedding, I don't believe it could offend anyone.'

Anesha nodded. 'To me it is a compliment to my culture that your sister wishes to include Sri Lankan traditions.'

Zoe nodded. 'Thank you, Anesha.'

'What sort of colours would your sister like?'

A discussion commenced and ended with, 'Give me five minutes and I'll have a selection for you.' Calling for help, Anesha walked away.

True to her word, she arrived back a few minutes later and Zoe gave a small gasp. 'They are all utterly beautiful.' The eclectic mix of colour and whites, the delicacy of the beading and intricacy of the patterns whirled in her head as she tried to work out what her sister would like most. Turning to Matt, who had been silent throughout, she said, 'What do you think?'

'They are all beautiful; it's hard to say.' His tone was a little short and, as if he realised it, he smiled at Anesha. 'You have done such a good job it makes ours harder.'

'Perhaps you would like to try them on?'

Temptation beckoned and then Zoe shook her head. 'It wouldn't feel right—I don't want Beth to wear something I've actually worn. I know Beth will prefer something not too bright, so I think it's between this one and this one.' She pointed to two of them.

'I understand.' Anesha thought for a moment. 'If you like I can put them onto mannequins and then perhaps you will be able to see how each one will look and then you can choose.'

'That would be perfect.'

'And whilst I do that why don't you choose something for yourself?'

'I've got a dress that will probably work with either of the saris.'

To her surprise Matt shook his head. 'I agree with Anesha—you should choose something new, something chosen to complement Beth's dress. For the photos, for your memories... I think it's important.' He looked round the shop. 'It doesn't have to be a sari—or perhaps it should be.'

Anesha gestured to another shop assistant. 'Leela will help you, if you like.'

Ten minutes later Zoe surveyed herself in the mirror. 'I love it,' she breathed. The sari was a shimmering grey material shot through with threads of silver, and it made her feel almost magical. She liked too that it was both subtle and special—

'Would you like to show your partner?'

'No. I mean, he isn't my partner. He's the best man and I'm the bride's sister. So he doesn't need to see it.'

But it was more than that. She didn't want him to see it now—because, truth be told, Zoe wanted to knock Matt's socks off the next day.

Back in her normal clothes, Zoe followed Leela out and gave a small gasp when she saw the mannequins. 'Oh. They're both beautiful.' She looked at Matt. 'How are we going to decide?' After she had walked round five times Matt came over and gestured to a chair. 'OK. Close your eyes and picture tomorrow. What do you see?'

'Beth in the dress on the left.'

'Then that's the one we get.'

'Thank you.'

As they walked out of the shop Zoe glanced at Matt. 'You were very quiet in there.'

'There wasn't any need for me to say anything. So where are we going now?'

'To try and sort out the cake. I spoke to the bakery who were going to do it and they said we could pop in and they'd see what they can do. I'm pretty sure we can walk from here.'

'Sure.'

Zoe glanced at him, sure she could see trouble in his eyes.

'Is something wrong?' She halted. 'Didn't you like the sari? You should have said. If you think Dylan won't like it or Beth or—'

'Whoa. It's not that. That sari is perfect.'

'Then what is it?'

His steps slowed. 'It's just. I was just…' He rocked backwards on his heels. 'I'm sorry,' he said.

'Sorry about what?'

'That you didn't have a proper wedding day. A chance to choose a dress with your sister. A chance to choose a dress at all. I should have thought at the time, instead of rushing you into it.'

She could hear genuine regret in his voice and she laid a hand on his arm.

'Please don't feel bad. If I'd wanted any of those things I would have said so. I was there, remember? But it wouldn't have felt right to have gone for a traditional wedding. We were getting married for the baby's sake. We barely knew each other. With hindsight we were fools to do it.' Only it hadn't felt like that—it had felt magical, as though she could finally put tragedy behind her, lay the ghosts of the past down and start a new chapter of her life. With a man she'd believed had wanted the baby as much as she had, welcomed the idea of family. 'But it was our decision, foolish or not,' she said. Though, really, if anyone had been the fool it had been her. She'd heard what she wanted to hear, seen what she'd wanted to see.

'In the end it doesn't really matter. Our marriage was brief and ill-fated, so what we wore on the day of our wedding doesn't really matter.'

'You wore a floral dress with daisies on it,' he said. 'And you tucked a carnation in your hair.'

'You remember.'

'Every minute of it and, for what it's worth, you looked stunning.' He hesitated. 'It may not have been conventional, or traditional, but we were happy.'

In that moment Zoe was no longer standing in the shade of trees on a Sri Lankan island... Instead she was back to her wedding day four and a half years ago.

'Do you remember our wedding lunch?'

'You said you had a craving for proper fish and chips.'

'So after the register office you drove us down to Brighton.' She inhaled and it was almost as though she could smell the tang of salt, hear the cries and shouts from Brighton pier. 'We had proper fish and chips on the beach.' Her tastebuds tingled with the remembered tang of the salt, the vinegar, the crisp, cooked-to-perfection batter. She could hear the swish of the waves and see the soar of the seagulls. Feel the smooth bumpiness of the pebbles under her toes.

After lunch they'd paddled in the sea and then wandered round the city hand in hand, bought each other silly souvenirs from the shops, ended up starting their honeymoon in Brighton.

'No matter what happened after, that day was magical.'

And so had the night been. Memories cascaded over her, her body shivered with remembered pleasure and a bittersweet desire that culminated in an unstoppable urge to step forward now, to place her hand on his chest, to feel his strength under her fingertips, to stretch up on tiptoe and brush her lips against his…and then she was lost.

Lost in him, in his smell, his taste…in the glorious escape of his lips as they locked onto hers in an inevitable, wonderful kiss that wove a sensory magic that engulfed her in a sheer maelstrom of pleasure that sent a surge of desire through her body, that twisted and clenched her tummy with a yearning for more as his hand slid down her back and she pressed against him.

It was the caw of a bird that brought her to her senses. *Whoa.* What the hell was she doing? How much of an idiot was she? Somehow from somewhere she found the strength to pull away, and stared up at him aghast. Anger—with herself, with him—caused her already ragged breathing to catch further and she stepped backwards.

'Zoe.' His voice was jagged, almost hoarse. 'I—'

'Don't say anything. That was stupid, triggered by something that was never real. Our wedding day wasn't magical or, if it was, it was an illusion.'

'That isn't true. It was real, Zoe. All of it.'

Anger deepened as she shook her head in disbelief. 'How can you say that? You didn't want to get married. You didn't want a family. You didn't want the baby. You married me because you thought it was the right thing to do.'

'Yes, I did. But I wanted it to work. I believed we could make it work. I believed we could be happy together.' Now he stepped towards her. 'You are right—I hadn't planned to have a baby... *We* hadn't planned that. But I wanted to be a good father.'

'But you would just have been making the best of it—it wasn't what you wanted to do with your life.'

'It wasn't what I planned to do with my life—but sometimes plans change. You can't always control what happens, but you can try and control what happens next. I had no regrets about the baby, Zoe. From the minute I knew you were pregnant I wanted to do right by him or her and I won't apologise for that. That is what I wanted to do with my life.'

Zoe looked up at him, saw sincerity in his dark eyes, but saw a darkness as well, a shadow that made her want to reach out to him, to soothe the demon she could see there.

She knew he spoke truth. It had been Matt who had urged the marriage—why would he have done that if he hadn't wanted to be part of the baby's life? He could have offered maintenance and weekend visitation rights, but he'd wanted to be there properly. Wanted to give the baby exactly what she had wanted to—a family. He'd also been willing to sacrifice his own dreams, his own plans, and had been willing to do that without complaint. So perhaps she should let her anger go.

She shook her head. 'I understand that,' she said. 'But I feel stupid. I believed you wanted what I wanted.'

'I did. I wanted us to be a family.' His voice was taut with sadness now.

'But not enough to try for another baby.' That was the bottom line and that was unanswerable.

'I…' Now the shadows darkened his eyes further and she could see the depth of pain there, one she couldn't fathom or understand. Then it was gone, like the cliched shutter clanging down. 'No. Not enough for that. But I swear to you, Zoe, I would have done all I could to be a good father if life had turned out that way. And…I swear to you that I grieved for our baby.'

Again, she heard sincerity, knew that again

he spoke truth, and she felt the last vestiges of rancour dissipate. 'I know you did,' she said softly, and now she did step closer to him and gently placed her hand on his arm, took comfort when he covered it with his own. 'But it was a long time ago.' Her glance caught the dial of his watch. 'And now we have a cake and flowers to sort out.' She hesitated. 'Unless you think we shouldn't do this together after what happened.' The kiss, the aftermath of which was still buzzing inside her. But... 'I promise you it won't happen again. It was a moment of stupidity.'

'Agreed. And we shouldn't let that moment stop Project Wedding. Not when we have so little time left.'

'OK. Let's go. The cake shop isn't far, then we'll go to the bazaar for the flowers.'

Half an hour later, cake sorted, they entered the bazaar and Matt gazed around, tried not to get swept away by the hustle and bustle of the crowds of shoppers, the mishmash of stalls selling an assortment of wares, from brightly coloured fruits and vegetables to exotic swathes of materials.

A chaos that matched his thoughts; he was still knocked for six by the kiss they'd shared, his body still alive from the zing of desire.

But he was also fazed by the conversation, loathed the idea that Zoe believed their marriage had been based on a foundation of lies.

Perhaps hated more the shades of grey that meant he couldn't explain the truth to her. That the reason he didn't want a baby was his own inadequacies, that his greatest fear in their marriage was that he would let them down. That when she'd lost the baby, the grief had dredged up an older grief, had mixed and swirled with the loss of his baby brother until he couldn't think straight.

All he knew was that he couldn't go through that sort of loss again, that he couldn't risk that sort of responsibility. After all, why hadn't he done something to save his brother? Why couldn't he even remember him? Why hadn't he raised an alarm? Told someone. Run out on the street and proclaimed it. Maybe because he'd been too busy looking out for himself.

Enough. He couldn't change the past. Not what he'd done aged five or aged twenty-six. Telling Zoe wouldn't change the past either. Nothing could.

'Matt? Are you OK?'

'I'm fine. Just getting my bearings.' A sensation alien to him; he was always in control. It was a defining feature of his character. Perhaps with that control came a certain emptiness, but that was fine with him. So he had to be careful, careful not to let Zoe in. So there could be no more kisses.

Zoe glanced down at her phone. 'I think the flower stall I want is over that way.' She pointed and he nodded.

'If we get separated, let's meet up back at the entrance. But in the meantime maybe hang on to the loop of my jeans. Or…' He held out his hand. 'It makes sense to hold hands. That way we won't get separated and waste time having to fight our way back to the entrance.'

She looked at his hand for a while, then nodded, placed her hand in his, and he tried not to react to the sheer familiarity of it. The memories of times gone by when holding Zoe's hand was as natural as breathing. But now it was simply for efficiency as they wended their way through the bazaar. Efficiency. Efficiency. Efficiency. A mantra on repeat until they reached the flower stall.

Scent and colours exploded onto his sensory fields; heaps and piles of exotic blooms and greens exuded a medley of fragrance. The smiling owner stepped forward.

'How can I help you?' he asked, his English accented but fluent.

'My sister is getting married tomorrow, at the hospital. I'd like to decorate the room with flowers and create a floral arch that they can stand under for the actual ceremony. They need to smell enough to mask the hospital smell but not be too overwhelming. I also need a bouquet for the bride to hold and I want the whole thing to be full of life and vibrancy and happiness.'

'OK. Then this is what you need.' The man took a quick glance round the stall and tables and then, with impressive speed, he gathered together a sample of flowers. 'For the arch. And then these for the bouquet. And what about for the bride's hair and your own?'

'I don't think I'd know how to arrange flowers in someone's hair.'

'It's easy. Do you have a phone?'

'Well, yes…'

'Then I will instruct your man how to do it, my son will video it and tomorrow you will know how to do it.'

'I…' Matt saw the frantic look she cast at him and man did he sympathise.

'Your sister—she will look amazing.'

'If that's OK with you, Matt?'

It was almost comical. *Almost.* The fact that two adults were both in a spin at the prospect of him braiding her hair. This wasn't

personal. Hairdressers did it all the time—
and he would not admit to anyone that he was
loth to do something so simple. 'Of course,'
he said.

'OK. I will do it for my daughter and you
will follow what I do. My son will video us
and tomorrow you simply need to follow the
video. It is easy. Really easy.'

Easy. Really easy. Matt tried to keep the
words in the forefront of his mind for the next
twenty minutes, all too aware that his expression, her expression, were being captured on
screen. But, damn it, it wasn't easy.

As he separated her hair into three parts,
his fingers skimmed the nape of her neck
and he felt the shiver run through her body,
tried not to recall exactly how sensitive her
neck was, how much she'd loved him to trail
kisses…

Easy. Really easy, Matt.

As his fingers twined in the silken tresses
of her hair, memories awakened of all the
other times he'd run his fingers through her
hair, washed it for her when they'd shared a
shower, the times when he'd woken to have
it tickle his nose…

It was a sort of exquisite torture for both
of them. The tautness of her body gave her
away. Until finally it was over and he stepped

back, managed a smile at the approving nod of the stall owner.

'Very fine job,' he said. 'Tomorrow the bride will look beautiful and so too will her sister. Come early and all the flowers you need will be ready.'

Zoe rose to her feet and he saw her sway slightly as though perhaps her legs were trembling in sheer desire, saw her pull herself together. 'Thank you very much. For everything. You have been wonderful.'

'It is our pleasure.' The man beamed at them. 'My great-grandfather started this stall many, many years ago, and his motto was always that happy customers make a happy business.'

As they walked away she raised her hand to touch her hair. 'I'm sorry if it was uncomfortable.'

'It wasn't.'

Zoe came to an abrupt stop and half turned, gave a gasp of surprise.

'What's wrong?' Matt, wrong-footed, stopped.

'I saw your pants catch fire,' she quipped, and he couldn't help it—he laughed.

'OK. Maybe I lied. Maybe it was a little awkward.'

'Just a bit, right?' Now she laughed too and

as they started walking again he felt a pit-pat in his chest as he watched the grace of her walk, inhaled the sweet fragrance of the flowers woven into the vivid red of her hair.

'What next?' he asked.

'I want to pick up some material from one of the stalls to decorate the walls with, and I thought I'd pick up some food and we could make dinner tonight? That way we can go over the preparations for tomorrow and make sure we haven't forgotten anything.'

'Sounds good.'

Memories of the first heady months of their relationship, before Zoe had discovered she was pregnant, before he'd rushed her into marriage, before the miscarriage, popped into his head. Memories he hadn't thought of for years—the good ones submerged by the dark shadows of the final weeks of their marriage and the jagged pain of its end.

The days when she'd come round to his flat armed with various ingredients, when they'd taken it in turns to pick new recipes and cooked together, the laughter, the fun, the times the cooking had been abandoned halfway through as attraction had simmered alongside the meal.

But that was then, and this was now. This dinner had an agenda of a different sort. Yet as they chose the vegetables…the jackfruit and sweet potatoes…anticipation grew inside him, even as he told himself it was pointless, dangerous, stupid…

CHAPTER SIX

ZOE LOOKED ROUND the kitchen and tried to quell the sense of excitement, knew it was stupid and inappropriate. They'd spent the whole of the previous evening figuring out how wrong they were for each other. A conclusion that was supposed to have knocked attraction on the head.

So why wasn't it working? Matt was one hundred per cent not her Mr Right. Wouldn't even make it to first-date status. But…her body hadn't got the memo. Worse, though, was the fact that she'd enjoyed today, enjoyed his company, enjoyed being with him. She closed her eyes, knew that she had to be careful; she would not tread the same road as before. Couldn't let attraction and liking con her into believing they had a future. It hadn't worked last time and there was no way it could work now—not when she knew he didn't want a long-term relationship or a family. So to fall for the illusion this time would be beyond foolish—she had a plan, a life plan, and she wouldn't let Matt derail it.

But no amount of common sense could stop her heart from giving a hop, skip and a jump when he entered the kitchen. Shirtsleeves rolled up, hair spiky, his brown eyes warm and relaxed, and the way he looked at her brokered memories of the past.

No, no, no!

'Perfect timing,' she said brightly. 'I've got all the ingredients together. Do you want to chop or cook?'

'I'm at your service. I'm happy to do either.'

'You chop.' That way she could concentrate on the cooking and noting down the recipe to see if it was worthy of adding to her restaurant list.

Though soon enough she figured she'd got it wrong. There was something so goddamn sexy about a man chopping up vegetables, especially the way Matt was. Deft, competent, quick, and now she couldn't drag her eyes away from the lithe strength of his fingers, the sturdiness of his wrists, the smooth sculpture of his forearm.

'Ouch…' That was what happened when

you got distracted—she'd completely taken her attention off the pan and it spat oil at her.

Quickly she turned the heat down and turned to find him next to her. 'Hey, are you OK?'

'I...I'm fine. Honestly. I had the heat on too high and I...' The words shrivelled on her lips because right now all she could focus on were his lips, his face, the way he had taken her hand and stretched the palm out to look at it. Heat flushed her whole body and she was pretty sure it had nothing to do with the spicy scent of the chillies. 'I'm fine.'

Hell and damnation. She had to stop this now. Using every effort of will, she gently pulled her hand away and turned towards the oven and Matt stepped back hurriedly, as if he too realised the danger proximity brought.

'Good. Well, here are the first of the ingredients.'

And soon the kitchen was imbued with the scent of garlic and onions, the sizzle of chilli and ginger.

'Smells amazing,' she managed, but knew too that she wasn't only talking about the food. Because as they worked together, adding the ingredients with care, the pumpkin, beans, the raw banana and the coconut milk, it was impossible not to occasionally brush against each other, not possible not to be close enough that she could smell him, that elusive whiff of expensive soap and sheer Matt. That made her want to move closer, move in, snuggle against the hardness of his chest, feel his arms around her...

'I... Sorry, you'll need to chop some extra ingredients—we need to temper the curry. It's like the final step. It adds that extra layer of spice and intensity of taste.' But now the words took on a different meaning, and she wanted, craved, something more than food, a different type of spice, another type of intensity.

'No problem,' he said, his voice deep, and she could feel heat flush her body.

So it was almost a relief when her phone rang...a relief moderated by anxiety when she saw that it was her mum. *It's OK.* Of course they would be able to spend a few hours on a video call. For Beth's wedding. No way could this be a cancellation call. Not when her mum knew she needed to be there.

'Hi, Mum. Thank you for calling me back. I just wanted to go through the timings for tomorrow and what you need to do.'

'Actually, darling, there's been a bit of a problem.'

'What sort of a problem?' Zoe moved into

the corner of the kitchen, turned slightly away from Matt as she listened.

'Your dad's been asked to make a speech at the start of the protest march. It's a great honour and of course a great responsibility and it means that we'll be on the road at the time of the ceremony.'

'But…surely someone else could make the speech? Perhaps Dad could write it and—'

'That wouldn't feel right, darling. This may even be televised, garner a lot of press—he can't shirk that duty. He has a chance to make a real difference.'

'But what about Beth? It will make a huge difference to her whether you are there. Or maybe Dad could go and you could be there.'

'No, your dad needs me by his side. And we know too that we brought you girls up to put others before yourselves. If your dad's speech can potentially change the mind of people about the climate, then it could make a difference that actually impacts on the planet. If Emmeline Pankhurst had stayed at home to attend to family matters women wouldn't have the vote today.'

As always, a sense of hopelessness prevailed, a sense that actually she was being selfish, that Zoe was a bad person to expect her parents to put family above the greater good.

Her mum said, 'There. I knew you wouldn't disappoint us. Please explain to your sister and send us photos. Love to everyone and your dad sends love as well.'

Zoe put the phone down and tried to quell the rage inside her. What she now wanted to do was break things, anything. But she wouldn't, couldn't. She'd vowed all those years ago after Tom's death to turn her life around and not let her parents get to her.

But right now that was hard, when it was Beth who would be hurt.

'Hey. Is everything OK?' She could hear the concern in his voice and she forced her face into neutral with a hint of bright.

'Absolutely fine. Sorry about that. I'll put the rice on and then we can eat.'

'Zoe. Don't.'

'Don't what?'

'Don't pretend you're OK. I can tell you're not.'

'I said I'm fine.'

'And I can see that you're not. I'd like to help.'

'I don't want to talk about it.' Somehow she needed to get the anger under control, the anger and frustration and disappointment and confusion.

'Fair enough.' He glanced round the room,

walked over to a sofa and picked up a cushion, walked back and held it up.

'What are you doing?'

'You look like you'd like to hit something. Why not this? Seeing as I don't think there is a punchbag handy. It's OK to be angry—whatever it is you're angry about. Take it out on the cushion.'

Her mother's voice echoed in her ears, the time-worn excuses she'd heard time and again, and perhaps *she* could accept them, but not when they were going to hurt her sister. Lovely, kind, loving Beth, who never asked anyone for anything, who had been the perfect daughter whilst Zoe had run amok. She deserved more. The anger roiled.

Matt moved out to the centre of the room and held the pillow up. 'Go for it.'

Zoe eyed the cushion; at first she felt stupid, as though she was making a colossal fool of herself, but as he stood there, his face neutral, no judgement and not even a hint of a smile on his lips, the pillow held straight out, she shrugged. Stepped forward and lashed out.

Her first attempt was soft, still fuelled by the idea of ridicule.

'That's it, but you can hit it as hard as you like. Don't worry about feeling silly—

channel the feelings, the anger, the frustration, the lack of control...whatever it is that's making you mad. Take it out on the cushion, then it doesn't have to be inside you.'

Zoe nodded. The hell with it. *Wham-wham-wham.* She slammed her fist into the cushion time and again. Each thud reverberated and for a few minutes she was lost in the sensation; the satisfaction of venting and focusing her anger did help, and finally she stopped, dropped her hands to her sides and looked at him, her breath still coming fast.

'That really did work. I feel...better, though I'm not sure why. It hasn't changed anything.' He dropped the pillow onto the sofa. 'Why do I get the feeling you've done this before?'

'I have. I'm not a counsellor, but sometimes I do work with the kids at the foundation, only under guidance, of course. Some of the kids are so angry and they can't or won't or just don't want to talk about it. That anger can lead to them punching walls and hurting themselves. So we try to help them by telling them it's OK to be angry and finding a different way to let it out. Sometimes we take them somewhere outdoors so they can scream and shout and swear. Some people like obstacle courses or massive ball pits and throwing things. Others prefer punchbags.

But a cushion works too. It's a physical outlet so the anger doesn't fester so much inside you, because that's the worst of it, isn't it? It feels like you can't change it, can't control it, can't do a damn thing.'

The way he spoke the words showed an understanding that ran deep on personal levels—she knew it and the question tumbled from her lips: 'You've felt it, haven't you? Punched walls, been angry.'

He hesitated, then nodded. 'Yes. It's a long time ago, but, yes, I've punched a wall or two.' On impulse she reached out and took his hands in hers, turned them over and saw the light scars on his knuckles, ran a finger gently over them. Wondered what had triggered his anger. 'The wall won,' he said, his smile rueful. 'That's why cushions are better. They put up less resistance. And once you've released the anger that then frees you to try and consider the situation from a different perspective. Sometimes there's a solution you couldn't see before, sometimes there's nothing you can do but accept it and move on.'

'I thought I had accepted it,' Zoe said with a sigh. She walked over to the counter and stirred the curry. Saw that he had started the rice.

'Do you want to talk about it?' he asked.

'You don't have to, but if you think it would help?'

'I…' As she looked at him Zoe realised she did want to. After all, it was hardly a secret—she would have to tell him anyway. Perhaps telling him would make it easier to break the news to Beth. 'That was my mum. They aren't going to be able to attend the ceremony tomorrow even by video.'

'Why not?' His tone was non-judgemental.

'For the same reason they couldn't get on a flight. A cause. They are in the midst of participating in an environmental protest, a proper organised march through London, various sit-ins, et cetera. Dad's now been asked to make a speech in central London and he feels it's his duty to do it.' She shook her head. 'Actually, no, that's not true. He wants to do it.'

'Instead of being there for his daughter?'

Zoe nodded. 'They believe the cause is more important than the individual. It's always been like that and I know it's wrong but sometimes it makes me angry. I used to be angry for myself—I wanted them to come to sports days, to concerts, even to parent-teacher evenings. But this time I wanted them to be there for Beth, to put Beth first and stuff the cause. Which probably makes me a bad person.' Or an even worse person than she already was. Her attitude, her behaviour, her neediness to win her parents over, had cost a life. She had been the one to take Tom to the dark side and then she'd left him there. And she couldn't blame her parents for that.

'Of course it doesn't. You are not a bad person, Zoe. Your parents have a duty to you and Beth. More than a duty—they should want to be there for her.'

'They do. But they believe what they want is less important than doing what is right.'

'To me, that doesn't make sense. They could do both. Someone else could make the speech. They chose to have a family— that means their family should come first. They should have come to your school sports events, your graduation and everything else.'

His words were a reminder of his own decision—to not have a family. Because he knew he couldn't put them first, that his foundation came first. The way he'd spoken about the kids and their anger, the way he empathised with them, showed her how much they mattered to him. And she couldn't help but wonder what had sparked that. He'd told her so little about his childhood, other than his parents had died when he was young and he had gone into care. That he'd had good carers and been lucky. Now she wondered, realised that they'd both drawn veils over their childhoods, relegated the past to the past. Maybe that had been a mistake.

'And I'm sorry they didn't, sorry they aren't going to be part of Beth and Dylan's wedding. But…perhaps Beth won't be as hurt as you think. It sounds as though it won't be a surprise.'

'I know. But some of the Sri Lankan traditions do centre around the mother-daughter relationship and…' Frustration wobbled her voice. 'Just once I wanted Mum to come through.'

'Can you take your mum's place?'

'No. I'm the younger sister—but it's not even that. Beth has always been the one who looked after me. It was Beth who worked out how to cook pasta, how to push a chair over to the stove. Beth worked out how to use a tin opener so we could have baked beans on toast or spaghetti hoops. Beth looked after me.' Whilst all she'd done was shout and rage and seek attention.

'Beth did what any good older sibling would do.' There was an edge to his voice and she studied his expression, saw the grim set of his lips. 'But I bet you were there for her too.'

'I...' Zoe stopped and said slowly, 'I tried. But I wasn't very good at acceptance and getting on with it. I tended to shout and scream and yell and I suppose that did sometimes achieve something. It did sometimes jolt Mum and Dad into doing things they would simply have forgotten otherwise. And I did look out for her at school.'

'Sometimes you have to scream. It sounds like you and Beth worked as a team.'

Zoe nodded. 'We did. We did everything together even if we did it differently. Until...' She broke off. Until she'd decided to go a step further for her parents' attention, until she'd taken rebellion several steps too far. 'Until we got older. But we are still really, really close.'

'Then the most important person for Beth tomorrow is you. And you will be there and you have done her proud—really you have. It's sad that your parents are as they are, but you can't change that. But what you have done is make tomorrow special for your sister. So do not beat yourself up that your parents won't be there. That's on them, not you. OK?'

'OK.' She hesitated. 'And thank you. For helping me put it all in perspective.' Reaching out, she touched his hand. 'And I'm sorry— for whatever made you punch walls.' She allowed a hint of a question to imbue the words, but wasn't surprised when his face closed off, as though perhaps he regretted his earlier admission.

'It's OK. It was all a long time ago. Water under the bridge.' But Zoe wondered, wondered if their belief that the past didn't matter was truly valid. Gently he pulled his hand away. 'Now how about we eat and make sure we're ready for tomorrow?'

'Good plan.'

CHAPTER SEVEN

EARLY THE NEXT MORNING, Matt entered the kitchen to find Zoe already up and ready. Her hair pulled back in a ponytail, dressed in cut-off trousers and a T-shirt, she looked ridiculously pretty, silhouetted against the beauty of the Sri Lankan sunrise.

'We can pick up breakfast at the market,' she said. 'I really fancy a freshly made egg hopper. If you don't mind going straight away.'

'Perfect.' And it was—Matt had something he wanted to do at the bazaar, an idea that had come to him the previous night after their conversation. He studied her expression, saw anxiety in her eyes. 'Hey. Don't look so worried. You've got this. We've got this. Beth and Dylan are going to have a happy wedding. Truly. And we're in this together, OK? Now let's get the flowers and then go and transform the hospital room.' He moved closer, tried not to be distracted by her proximity. 'Beth is lucky to have a sister like you.'

For a moment sadness panged through him as he wondered what would have happened if his baby brother had survived—would they have formed a bond, or would Matt quite simply have felt nothing? Did the fact his parents hadn't bonded with him mean he had no ability to bond with others? How he wished he had done for Peter what Beth had done for Zoe—worked out a way to look after him.

'Right. Let's go.'

Fifteen minutes later the driver dropped them at the bazaar and they climbed out. 'You head to the flower stall. I need to go and get something. I'll explain later.'

Twenty minutes later he returned to find the car brimming with sweetly scented delicate blooms creating a veritable blaze of colour.

'Wow.'

'They're beautiful, aren't they?' Zoe said. 'But now spill. Where did you go?'

As the car drew away Matt had a sudden qualm. Maybe he shouldn't have gone off and done this without consulting Zoe.

'Matt?'

'I had an idea. I looked up some Sri Lankan wedding traditions and there's one where the brother of the groom gives the bride a necklace to welcome her into the family. I realise Dylan hasn't got a brother, but I thought maybe David could do it, and I thought maybe as Beth's sister you could do the same and give Dylan something. That way you as a sister are performing a ceremony even if your mother isn't.'

He paused for breath and studied her face, saw tears sheen her eyes. 'That is...' She sniffed. 'It's made me want to cry. It's a perfect idea.'

He shifted on the seat, a mixture of pleasure that he'd got it right mixed with a sense of embarrassment at the praise.

'I'm glad you're pleased, but it's no big deal. I hope you approve of what I got as well.' He reached into the bag and pulled out two boxes. 'I didn't want it to be too personal, more symbolic, so this is what I settled on.' He showed her the cufflinks, a simple circular design made of white gold and onyx, for Dylan, and the brooch he'd chosen for Beth, a delicate leaf design of gold.

'They will love them and they are beautiful.' She picked up her phone. 'I'll call Edwina and slot this bit into the ceremony as well.' She glanced at him. 'She's been great.'

'Yes. She is a lovely person.' Matt wondered if he should mention he'd been in touch with Edwina about the orphanage and decided not to. He understood now Zoe's reluctance to get involved with or engage in any sort of cause. Now he knew more about her parents so much more made sense. Especially her need to find a man who was a good father, who would put his family first. The box Matt could most emphatically never tick, but what he could do was be here now and make this wedding a success. 'Let's get this show on the road,' he said.

A lovely nurse greeted them at the hospital and showed them to the room where the ceremony would take place. 'I'm sorry it's so sterile, but it truly is the best room.'

'There is no need to apologise. We are so grateful the hospital agreed to the ceremony at all. And Beth and Dylan would like everyone to come and have cake later on.'

Matt turned to Zoe. 'I am in your hands. Instruct me and I will do whatever you ask.'

In truth he had no idea how to transform the clean but sterile room into anything approaching festive.

An hour later Matt looked round the room, hardly able to believe the transformation. The window was now the focal point with an arch of flowers skilfully arranged in a riotous, glorious assembly of colour and scent. Red mingled with white and twisted together to create the perfect backdrop. Drapes of gauzy material toned down the institution-coloured walls and added a touch of magic, and a trestle table in the corner held a beautifully decorated chocolate cake atop a snowy-white tablecloth covered in gold foil wedding bells.

'This is beautiful; I cannot believe you managed to make it this…magical.'

'We did it,' she said. 'I couldn't have done this on my own.'

'But it's your creation. I was just the…'

'Muscle…' she said and suddenly flushed as her gaze lingered on his shoulders and then she looked away. 'Now I'll go and help Beth get ready.' Her eyes widened in sudden anxiety.

'What's wrong?'

'How will I know how to do it? I mean, we saw it on the mannequin but—'

'Hey. Don't panic. I videoed Anesha putting the saris on the mannequins. I'll send you the video.'

'I take it back. You're not the muscle— you're the brains. Thank you.' Moving over to him, she brushed her lips against his cheek and the feeling of warmth that trickled through him was bittersweet. The urge to simply take her in his arms and hold her, to feel her head rest on his chest, was nigh on overwhelming. But he resisted, knew he needed to be careful, that he could not, would not, get involved with Zoe again. He couldn't give her what she wanted most in life and he mustn't forget that. Mustn't let her ignite the swirl and whirl of emotion that had sent him into a spin that had ended in pain and hurt and disillusionment four years before. Stepping back, she waved. 'I'll see you at the ceremony.'

Zoe smiled as Beth headed towards her, pushed all thoughts of Matt from her mind and moved forward to hug her older sister.

'Happy wedding day! I am sorry it's not how it was meant to be but—'

'It doesn't matter. Truly. We are so grateful David is alive and with us and the doctors are optimistic about his prognosis. And we are so happy to be getting married.' She stepped back, held Zoe's hands in hers. 'And thank you, Zo, with all my heart. For organising this.'

'You're welcome. I hope, really hope, I've got it right.'

'It couldn't be wrong.'

'And it wasn't just me. I couldn't have done it anywhere near as well without Matt.'

To her own annoyance she could feel heat touch her face as Beth studied her expression. 'Is there anything I should know?' her sister asked.

'Absolutely not. Definitely not. No.'

Beth raised her eyebrows. 'What was that quote again? Something about people who protest too much?'

'Not applicable here. All that has happened is that we had a proper talk, and we have decided to put the past behind us and focus on being civilised and polite so there is no awkwardness now or in the future.'

Aware of how stilted her words sounded, she frowned. 'Anyway, this is your wedding day. We don't have time to discuss Matt of all people.'

'OK. But…' Beth hesitated. 'Putting the past behind you is all well and good provided you've faced it and actually discussed it. You did, didn't you?'

'Um…sort of. But not really. You can't change the past. The past is gone, Beth. I don't want to revisit it.'

'Revisit or face?' Her sister's voice was gentle with no judgement.

'Same difference. But the most important

thing is Matt and I have agreed to be civil.'
Time to close this down. Beth looked way too
dubious and way too interested. 'Anyhoo…
It's time for you to get ready.' She pushed the
door open. 'Ta-da.'

Beth's eyes widened and she raised her
hand to her mouth on an intake of breath. 'It
is gorgeous. Beyond beautiful.'

'And it will look even better on you. Matt
videoed the shop assistant putting it on a
mannequin so we should be able to figure
it out. And we got a video of Matt braiding
flowers into my hair, so I know how to do
yours.'

'So you and Matt really did everything together.'

'Yes. He wanted to be part of it. We both
wanted this to be special for you and Dylan.
That's all.'

'Sure.' Beth nodded. 'And it will be, because you're here.'

'I am so sorry Mum and Dad aren't.'

'Don't be. It's not really that surprising and
I'd rather they weren't here than they came
grudgingly. Mum and Dad are who they are
and the best thing to do is simply have no
expectations of them. Because you know
what? *They* miss out—they miss out on us
and being a family. That's what Dylan's fam-

ily have shown me. What it's supposed to be like. They all look out for each other, but they are all good people as well. They do good things, but they believe family comes first. And for me you come first. I've got your back and you've got mine and nothing can change that.'

'Nothing,' Zoe agreed and hugged her sister. 'Now, let's get you ready.'

'Let's get us ready.'

Half an hour later they looked at each other in satisfaction. 'You look stunning,' Zoe said. The cream sari flowed in elegant waves of silken material, and Beth wore it with a grace and fluidity Zoe could only hope she emulated.

'So do you.' Beth smiled mistily as there was a knock on the door and seconds later Manisha entered.

'I came to see if I could help. And to thank you, Zoe, for all you have done.'

'I enjoyed every minute,' Zoe assured her.

'And you have done a wonderful job. Beth, you look…' the older woman's eyes filled with tears and she blinked fiercely '…very beautiful. I am so grateful to you. David is thrilled that the wedding is going ahead before his operation. As am I. I know he will go into the operation more at peace.'

Beth moved forward to hug her mother-in-law-to-be. 'He is going to be all right.'

'I know, but I also know, whatever happens, I have been so lucky to have been married to the love of my life.'

'Manisha and David got married three weeks after they met,' Beth told her sister.

'Yup.' Manisha smiled. 'It is hard to believe now, but back then we were young and we knew… I can't explain it, but we knew that what we had was real. And now here we are all these years later with a wonderful son who is about to marry a wonderful woman. And I believe that David will come through this. But whatever happens I am glad that we have spent every possible moment with each other.'

Zoe blinked back tears, rose and hugged the diminutive woman.

'If anything will help bring him through, it is the knowledge that you are here.'

'Thank you.' The older woman smiled. 'Now let's go. You are such a beautiful bride, Beth, inside and out, and my son is lucky.'

Zoe smiled, filled with genuine happiness for her sister, not only that she had found the man she loved, but that she had also been welcomed in by his family, was secure in the knowledge that she was truly loved. Would

anyone ever feel like that about her? Did she
even want them to? It didn't matter. Soon she
would start her search for Mr Right and that
was the right way forward for her. Her first
step towards a family.

Matt stood next to Dylan, saw the expression
on his best friend's face, the love as he looked
at his father. David smiled. 'Look at the door,
son,' he said. 'This is a moment you'll remember for the rest of your life.'

Matt glanced at the older man, relieved to
see that, although he had shadows under his
eyes, his skin held some colour and his voice
was strong. He'd insisted on wearing a shirt
and tie and he was seated to the side of the
window, love and pride on his face, his wife's
hand securely in his.

The love in the room, the sense of family
solidarity, was palpable and Matt felt a sear-
ing sadness that he'd never experience this,
never feel that bond. That for some reason
his parents hadn't had that basic primal love
for their children.

Then all such thoughts fled as the door
opened and Zoe and Beth came in. Perhaps
he should be focused on his best mate, on
the bride, but he wasn't. All he could see
was Zoe, dressed in a shimmering grey sari

shot through with silver; the glimpse of bare shoulder and the elegant flow of the material all complemented her natural beauty.

But it wasn't just the attire. It was the way she looked at Beth, the grace with which she walked, the brightness of her green eyes, flecked with happiness for her sister. Her glance went to Matt, snagged there; her focus was fully on him, and he hoped she saw the admiration in his eyes, admiration and desire and the fact that she had knocked his socks off.

And something lit in her eyes too, desire and also...perhaps a hint of wistfulness, for the memories, for the might-have-beens. For the fact that once they had embarked on this same journey and fallen at the first hurdle.

Seeing David's gaze rest on him, he pushed the thoughts away as futile and focused on the ceremony itself.

Edwina did an incredible job and everything went without a hitch. The whole ceremony was both seamless and moving, the mix of Western and Sri Lankan perfect, every vow and ritual conducted with love and meaning as Beth and Dylan promised to love each other for the rest of their days. The whole unleashed so many thoughts and in these beautiful moments Matt had a sudden wish that he could be different, could offer this rich deep relationship, and a sadness that his start in life, his own parentage, meant he couldn't.

Pushing away the thoughts, he tried to focus only on happiness for his friend. Reminded himself that he had turned his own life around, was a success, had wealth, a job he loved, a lifestyle he enjoyed, a foundation he believed in. His life was good and, as he'd told Zoe, he was perfectly content with shallow relationships full of fun.

So now he'd focus on the cake cutting, watching Beth and Dylan pose for a photo, radiant smiles on their faces.

Matt found himself next to Edwina and smiled at the celebrant. 'You did an incredible job. Thank you.'

'It is I who should be thanking you. What you are doing for the orphanage is wonderful.'

Matt shook his head. 'I want to show my appreciation to those kids that they were kind enough to release you for the morning. Organising a day out and donating some cricket gear isn't that big a deal.'

'It is to them. Half of them are cricket-obsessed.'

'I'd like to do something for the other half

too. But we can discuss that tomorrow when I come to see the orphanage.'

'We're all looking forward to it.' Edwina forked up the last bit of her cake. 'Now I need to shoot off to collect the minibus.'

As she headed off Matt caught a glimpse of silver out of the corner of his eye and turned to see Zoe, her gaze fixed on his face, and he wondered if she'd overheard the conversation. A question that was soon answered.

'That is kind of you. To donate cricket gear and organise a day out. When is it?'

'I'm not sure yet. I'm hoping to get a couple of the national cricket team to come along for a couple of hours. One of my clients is a big Sri Lankan cricket fan and sponsor so I'm hoping that will make a difference.'

'And you're visiting the orphanage too?'

'Yes, I want to thank the kids personally. And I want to see if my foundation can help the orphanage on a permanent basis. To do that I need to see for myself how the orphanage works before I commit any money to it.'

'What will it depend on?'

'Whether the whole organisation is legitimate—a lot of charities start out with excellent intent but then somehow paperwork, bureaucracy and downright dishonesty can take over. I know it sounds a bit ruthless, but I like to know the money I donate and raise genuinely helps the people who need it. Otherwise what's the point? I may feel good for being generous but that's not what it is all about.'

This he knew. There had been times as a child when he'd heard the praise heaped on his foster carers, when in fact he'd known they were in it for the money. Because he'd been the one given the cheap meals, the hand-me-down clothes, the room with the radiator turned off. Yet those carers had genuinely believed they were being good people to take him in at all.

'It doesn't sound ruthless at all,' she said. 'It sounds like the exact right thing to do. And I can hear how much you genuinely care.' She hesitated. 'Why didn't you tell me about all this?'

'I didn't want to distract you from the wedding preparations and I wasn't sure you'd want to hear about it. After what you told me about your parents, I can see that people with a big interest in a charitable cause must be problematic.'

She bit her lip and he could see trouble reflected in the green of her eyes as she shook her head. 'I do have mixed feelings about people with causes, but you're different. Everything you've just said shows me that. You're different from my parents—you've decided not to have a family because you want to prioritise your foundation.'

Matt focused on keeping his expression completely neutral as he processed her words. Zoe believed he didn't want a family because he believed his foundation was more important.

He was tempted to set the record straight, to say he fully believed you could do both, that her parents could have balanced their causes with their responsibilities as parents. After all, if they hadn't lost the baby that was exactly what Matt would have done. Again a glimpse of that future materialised and an ache for what could have been tugged inside him.

But that hadn't happened and wouldn't happen. In all consciousness he couldn't risk parenthood, yet, standing here next to Zoe, regret seeped through him. Regret and a sense of sadness. *Enough.* It was easiest to let Zoe believe what she believed. Best to focus now on helping the children he could help.

'I'll keep you posted on the orphanage from now on.'

'Actually, I was wondering if I could come with you when you visit. I'd like to thank the kids too. Without them all of this wouldn't have happened and that means a lot.'

'I'd like that.' Problem was, he suspected he liked it for all the wrong reasons: because it gave him another legitimate reason to spend time with Zoe.

At that moment Dylan rang a bell. 'Time for the speeches,' he said.

Zoe listened to the speeches, Matt's a perfect mix of serious and humour, David's short through necessity, but his words displayed dignity and a dry wit. Once he had finished Manisha stepped forward and Zoe saw Beth and Dylan exchange a look of surprise.

'My husband has asked that I also say a few more words,' Manisha said. 'We both wish to say thank you to Zoe and Matt for everything they have done. And we would like to give them a gift. Three days in Burati during the annual festival—it is a time of joy and significance and we think you will enjoy yourselves there. Have a holiday.'

Next to her David nodded and then spoke. 'It is important to me, to us, that you accept this gift.'

Zoe tried to think, her brain clouded with the sheer unexpectedness of the gesture. David and Manisha knew that she and Matt

were divorced—so why on earth would they
do this? A quick glance at Beth and Dylan
indicated they were as taken aback as Zoe
was. But what she could also see was that,
for whatever reason, this was important to
David. A man who was about to go into potentially life-threatening surgery.

So she wasn't surprised when Matt moved
next to her. 'We need to accept,' he mur-
mured. 'And sort it out later.'

With that he stepped forward.

'That is a very kind gift and we thank you
both very much.'

Soon after that the nurses and hospital staff
dispersed back to duties and, after a chat with
David and Manisha, Beth and Dylan headed
towards Zoe and Matt.

'We had no idea they were going to do
that,' Beth said.

'I know. But the point is, what are we supposed to do?'

Dylan sighed. 'I've just spoken to Dad. I'm
not sure if it's the medication, or something
to do with the operation, but he is adamant
he wants you to go. Says he owes it to Matt.'

Matt raised his eyebrows. 'He does remember Zoe and I are divorced?'

'Yup.' Dylan shook his head. 'I genuinely
don't get it, but he got quite agitated when we

tried to explain it may be awkward for you both.'

'I hope you told him we'll go,' Zoe said. 'The whole point of today was for everyone to be happy and for David to be at peace before the operation.' Manisha's face when she'd spoken of her husband filled her mind and on impulse she left the group as a nurse was getting ready to wheel David from the room.

'I wanted to thank you both for the gift,' she said. 'And tell David that we will go.'

'Is that a promise?' His voice was dry, held a hint of scepticism.

'It's a promise.' Looking up, Zoe saw that Matt was behind her, his voice deep and full of reassurance.

'Good.' The older man smiled, a smile that lit up his face. 'Then I'll see you on the other side.'

As he was wheeled from the room followed by his family Zoe looked at Matt. 'What are we going to do?'

Matt held her gaze. 'What do you want to do?' he asked softly.

His gaze held hers and she gulped, wanted to shy away from the truth. Because she wanted to go with him. Knew it was foolish, knew that in truth she couldn't even justify it. But that didn't mean she wasn't going to give it a damn good go.

'I think we have no choice. We have to go. We promised him, a man about to have a life-threatening operation. I don't think we can lie to him or renege.' She frowned. 'I just wish I understood why it mattered so much to him.'

Matt frowned. 'I don't know. Perhaps it *is* something to do with his medication, or perhaps it is simply a nagging feeling he owes me a debt for rescuing Dylan all those years ago. Whatever his reasoning, I think you're right. We'll have to go.'

Zoe tried to stem the stupid anticipation that welled up inside her. It was only a few days, one day at the orphanage and three in Burati. They had no choice; they couldn't refuse the wishes of a man about to enter the operating theatre for a bypass operation. Four days. It was nothing in the scheme of things.

'OK. It'll be fine,' she said brightly. 'It may even be fun.'

CHAPTER EIGHT

THE FOLLOWING DAY as the car travelled towards the orphanage Zoe watched the lush landscape whizz past and contemplated the day ahead. She was glad of the chance to thank the kids who'd helped make Beth's wedding possible. But she was also glad of this trip for other reasons.

She wanted to see Matt in action, physical proof that he had chosen this cause above family. A much-needed reminder of why Matt was not and could not be Mr Right. Because that was the best way to kill off any burgeoning feelings before they could take root. And she sensed if they were to spend more time together, then that was a must for her.

So today was the perfect way of showing common sense the futility of attraction to a man who had a cause.

As the car glided to a halt Zoe looked around at the group of houses in a large fenced area. The whole area looked welcoming and well kept. Curtains fluttered in the windows and plants were dotted around the doors in big heavy pots, the yard was well swept and there was a fenced-off garden that boasted a healthy-looking vegetable patch.

As they climbed out of the car Edwina came to greet them, a wide smile on her face. 'Thank you so much for coming.'

'It's no problem. I'm very happy to be here.'

'I thought you'd maybe like to look around, and then perhaps you'd join the kids for lunch.'

'That sounds perfect.'

The tour of the houses showed small but well-kept rooms. The rooms were shared but each child had their own designated area.

'I like that,' Matt said to Edwina. 'That everyone clearly has their own personal space.'

She nodded. 'I believe that is important. They need stability and as much as possible they need to know this is their home. Once here we do everything to make each child settle in and know that this is where they can stay until they are adults. When they do have to leave, I try, I really do, to help them to their next place. It is not as if they wake up on their eighteenth birthday and can look after themselves without support. But transition-ing is difficult.' She glanced at her watch. 'I am sorry but I will need to hand you over to Prisha now. She runs the kitchens. My shift at the local hospital starts soon. Any ques-tions, please ask and I'll do my best to help. This is a good place—I hope your founda-tion will help.'

They followed Edwina to the kitchen. 'This is Prisha. She is in charge of the kitchens and cooking.' Zoe smiled at the young woman, who was holding a toddler by the hand and an infant in a sling. She hoped she kept the expression of surprise from her face, but the young woman gave a soft laugh.

'I am young, but I am very good at what I do and I am also very grateful for the job. It is all thanks to Edwina.' She met Zoe's gaze. 'My story, I believe, is common throughout the world. My family are poor. They also be-lieve in some traditions and customs that I do not. I was married off and my marriage was not a happy one.' A shadow crossed her face and made Zoe want to reach out and hold her, and next to her she saw Matt's fists clench. 'In the end I left—I couldn't let anything happen to my children. The first time he hit Tomas I knew I had to leave. I was preg-nant and terrified. If my husband had caught me he would have killed me—I managed to hide aboard a cart. But Tomas cried. I was lucky. The driver did not take me back to my husband—instead he brought me here. I will be grateful to that man until my dying day. Now my babies will have a good life, without pain and fear. Edwina heard my story and she gave me sanctuary and offered me this job.'

Matt's body tensed beside her and she heard his intake of breath, knew he must be as moved as she was by this story.

The young woman shook her head. 'Do not look so sad. My story is a happy one, with a good ending. But now let me show you the kitchens. Tomas and I will show you. But first would you also like to see Adam?'

She tugged the sling open and Zoe saw the beauty of the baby and felt a profound gratitude that this one's innocence would be intact, hoped that Tomas couldn't and didn't carry any memories of his start, blessed the courage of this woman and the man who had helped her.

As they went round the kitchen, which was clean and organised, listening to Prisha explain how she devised the menu and encouraged the children to help, Zoe asked questions, impressed by how versatile the young woman was.

'But I would like more varied recipes.'

'Perhaps I can help. I'd love to come up with some new stuff for you to try.'

'I'd like that.' Prisha smiled.

It was only then that it occurred to Zoe how quiet Matt had been on this part of the tour; she really hoped he wasn't questioning Prisha's capabilities to do the job. An anxiety that increased as she saw how closed his face was. Perhaps Prisha shared her concern as at the end she turned to Matt. 'I hope you like what you've seen?'

'Absolutely. I think you are doing a wonderful job. My only concern is whether two children and this is too much for you.'

'No. Truly it isn't. I still have plenty of time with Tomas and Adam. The kids all help out as well. Tomas sees them all as family. Truly, it is not too much at all.'

'I'm glad and, as I said, I think you are doing a fantastic job.'

His smile was warm, yet Zoe sensed his tension, saw that his hands were slightly clenched, watched his fingers unfurl as they made their way from the kitchen towards the dining area, where two large trestle tables were surrounded by benches where about twenty children ranging in age from about seven to seventeen sat, eyeing their arrival with curiosity.

Matt moved to the head of the table, once again completely at ease, and Zoe wondered what it had been about Prisha that had caused him to tense up.

'I won't do a big speech. Zoe and I just wanted to thank you for the loan of Edwina yesterday. My friend and his fiancée were able to get married thanks to your kindness and I'd like a way to say a big thank you. For the cricket lovers amongst you I've arranged a trip to a match, and you'll get to meet the national team afterwards and have a knock around with them.'

There was a general outcry of sheer joy and Zoe couldn't help but smile as she saw the dazed happiness on the faces of most of the tables' occupants. Most but not all, and Matt continued.

'Now, I know that there may be among you a few who are not cricket fans—if so, please feel free to come and have a chat to me and I can work out another way to thank you.'

The lunch was delicious, fresh and aromatic and the talk round the table was mostly cheerful, though she noticed Matt was involved in a conversation with one of the older boys, his face sullen and brooding.

There was a tug on her sleeve. 'Did he mean it?' Zoe smiled at the girl of about twelve, her hair in two tight plaits, a serious look on her face. 'Did the man mean it? That if we don't like cricket we can truly ask for something else?'

'Yes, he did.'

'Oh.'

The girl lapsed into silence and Zoe looked down at her. 'So I take it you don't like cricket?'

She shook her head emphatically.

'So what would you like to do?'

'I would like to go shopping and buy books. I've read all the books here. I love them. But I'd love some new books. One day I'm going to write a book. That's my dream. Ravima says there is no point to dreaming, but I think there is.'

A girl Zoe estimated to be sixteen or so turned. 'I didn't exactly say that, Nimali. I said some dreams have no chance of coming true.'

'But you still have to try,' Nimali persisted.

'Why bother? There is no point trying if you know there is no chance of success. Much better to accept your fate.' There was a bitterness in her voice.

Zoe wasn't sure if Ravima was aware, but

the surrounding conversations had tapered away and everyone was listening to the girl.

'Ravima is right. This is the life we were born to, and nothing can change that.' This came from the youth sitting next to Matt and there was no mistaking the harshness in his voice. 'Certainly not some stupid day out—it achieves nothing except to make you feel better about yourselves. Then you'll disappear and not give us another thought.'

'That is not what I meant, Chaneth,' Ravima said. 'It is kind of them to organise a day. But dreams bring only misery.'

Matt rose to his feet and Zoe saw the darkness shadow his eyes before he blinked the demons away.

'I believe there is nothing wrong with dreaming as long as you also keep yourself grounded in reality. My background is similar to some of yours. I ended up without parents, in care. I dreamt of success, of making it, and those dreams did help me escape from reality for a while. I dreamt of being a famous footballer, a world-famous chef… In the end my dream was to be successful. In the end I did make it.' He turned to Ravima. 'If you—' he gestured around '—if any of you want to come and tell me your dreams, your ambitions, I will give you advice. Some dreams may not be realistic, but you should all dare to dream. One day they may be possible.'

'Rubbish! You're wrong to say this stuff—you're just raising false hope.' Chaneth picked up his plate and smashed it on the floor before striding from the room.

Matt turned to everyone else, his voice even. 'The offer stands. Zoe and I will be in the office for a few hours this afternoon.'

With that he turned and left the room and Zoe followed him, half running to keep up as he strode down the hallway towards the office.

'Matt?'

But before he could reply they heard footsteps behind them and Ravima and Nimali came into the room.

'We wanted to say sorry and ask you not to be angry with Chaneth. He isn't a bad person and please don't take away the day out because of what he said.'

'Whoa.' Matt stepped forward. 'I am sure Chaneth is not a bad person. You have nothing to apologise for and of course I won't take the day away. But I would like to know what your dream is, Ravima. If you want to tell me.'

The teenager shrugged, her chin jutting out as if daring them to laugh. 'I want to be a lawyer.' She glanced away. 'I know it's stupid. I could barely read when I got here a few years ago.'

'But you can read way better now and you learnt English really quickly and I think there must be a way,' Nimali said.

Matt looked at them and his face softened. 'I think there is a way. I can't guarantee you will become a lawyer, Ravima, but I can look into a way to provide you with more educational opportunities that would put you on the path to achieving it.'

'Really? You would do that?'

'I promise I will try. I don't know how the Sri Lankan educational system works but I will at least see what may be possible.'

'And you will help Chaneth too?'

'If I can.'

The girls left the room and Zoe studied Matt's face, saw a sudden tiredness there, could guess its cause.

'Chaneth's outburst wasn't true.'

'Wasn't it?' he asked. 'Perhaps I shouldn't have said what I said about dreams; perhaps all I did do was give false hope.'

'I don't believe that.' Her voice was gentle now. 'You didn't tell everyone you could make all their dreams come true, you offered advice and told them to dare to dream. And that is right.'

'Morally yes, but practically... I don't know.' He rose to his feet. 'Would you hold the fort here whilst I go and see if I can find Chaneth?'

'Of course.'

Two hours later Matt walked slowly down the corridor, trying to school his expression into one of neutrality, wanting to hide the effect of the past few hours. He was used to meeting kids who'd been through a lot, but it didn't really get easier. Each story harrowed him, even as he took a deep satisfaction in being able to help. But sometimes even that couldn't erase the sadness or the pain he felt for each child for what they had gone through.

Of course, some stories affected him more than others, triggered memories of his own and highlighted his own past. Chaneth's was one of those. So too was Prisha's. When he'd seen her with her two children, something had twisted inside him. Once he and his brother would have been like those two, endangered by a parent. Or, in their case, both parents. And in their case there had been no rescue for Peter, just for Matt.

He pushed the door open and paused on the

threshold. Zoe was sitting at the desk, note-book open, pen in hand.

'Did you find Chaneth?'

'Yes.'

'Is he OK?' She shook her head. 'Stupid question. He obviously wasn't. But did you talk to him?'

'Yes.'

'You look upset. Do you want to talk about it?'

For a moment he almost did. But that wasn't the way he worked. Better to lock the emotion down, focus on work, focus on any-thing other than feelings. Plus, talking to Zoe was pointless—in a few days they would part ways. He didn't want to get used to having her around, could still remember the sheer depth, the dark ravine of pain of missing her the first time round. So distance was impor-tant.

'I'm good. I need to look at the books and records now and then we can head back.'

Hurt flitted across her face before she nod-ded. 'I'll go and see if I can help Prisha with dinner. Let me know when you're ready to leave.'

'Sure.'

To his relief all the paperwork showed that the orphanage was run well, with the residents' well-being clearly being the priority. Once done, he locked everything away and went in search of Zoe, halting on the threshold to the kitchen.

Zoe was holding the baby, looking down at him with such an expression of tenderness that something twisted in Matt's chest. This was how she would have looked at their baby. This was how his own mother had never looked at him.

Zoe looked up. 'Isn't he beautiful?' she said softly. 'Why don't you hold him?'

His heart hammered his ribcage even as he told himself not to be foolish. Forcing himself forward, he managed a smile, looked down at Adam and a memory zinged across his mind. Someone, some fuzzy figure, holding a baby out to him. 'Would you like to hold him?' The voice harsh, abrasive, with a mocking tone to it.

He stepped backwards, tried not to flinch. Was it a real memory or a fabrication of his imagination? 'He's gorgeous.' He forced the words out. 'But now we need to leave.'

CHAPTER NINE

ZOE GLANCED ACROSS at Matt as the car carried them back to the resort. He was looking down at his laptop, had apologised but said he wanted to get on with the work whilst it was all fresh in his mind.

Which Zoe knew to be nonsense. Put simply, Matt didn't want to talk to her. And, exactly as he had done in their marriage, he was using work as an excuse. The car pulled up at the resort and they climbed out. 'I'd better get on with this,' he said. 'But I'll be ready to leave bright and early tomorrow.'

'Cool,' she said, even as hurt touched her.

She bit her lip, aware that she'd simply assumed she and Matt would eat together, discuss the day's events, plan for the next few days.

Entering her villa, she opened the well-stocked fridge and stared at the contents. Closed the door and drummed her fingers on the worktop. Matt had been hurting, she knew that, had seen it and, damn it, she wanted to help him. Just as he had helped her. So this time she wasn't going to let him push her away.

Before she could change her mind she got up and headed to the door, exited her villa and walked down the path to his and knocked loudly on the door.

A couple of minutes and he answered.

'I'm going to cook an omelette and I wondered if you want some.'

'Thanks, Zoe, but I'm not hungry.'

He looked as though he was going to shut the door and she jumped in. 'OK. I lied. I'm not here about omelettes really. I thought you may want to talk. Or if you don't want to talk maybe you could use some company. Maybe I could hold the pillow and you could punch it. Or…I could sit in a corner and have a cup of cocoa.' She could see reluctance on his face. 'I opened up to you and it helped me. I'd like to return the favour.'

'You don't have to do that. I don't really do talking.'

'Fine, we won't talk. How about we go for a walk or a run? Along the beach. Perhaps a run would help.'

He looked down at her and then gave the smallest of smiles. 'You're not going to go away, are you?'

'Nope.'

'OK. Actually, a run sounds good.'

'Good.'

Five minutes later, both changed into shorts and T-shirts, they were jogging down to the beach, the evening temperature perfect, a breeze that countered the remaining heat from the day.

It didn't take long to settle into a rhythm, to work out how to run at the same pace. A sideways glance saw how easily he ran, each stride even and unlaboured as he pounded down the sand, and soon they were caught in the moment, the adrenalin of the exercise, the lap of the waves and the golden glint of the moonlight on the sand.

'Is it OK if we sprint the final bit?' he asked, and she nodded, sensed he needed to let go, to pound out his feelings and his emotions.

Soon the sand flew under their feet and she watched as he headed away from her, running as though there were demons at his back, and she wondered if in fact there were exactly that. Couldn't help but admire the beauty of him in action, the strength of his back, the muscular strength of his legs, the ripple of thigh muscle, the movement of his arms.

She shivered as he eventually slowed down

into a jog and she caught up with him as he came to a stop and sank down onto the sand. She dropped down next to him and he turned.

'Thank you,' he said. 'I needed that.'

'I'm not surprised.' She drew a pattern in the sand. 'I didn't expect it, but, spending time at the orphanage, I liked those kids. A lot. Enough that I care.'

'It happens,' he said.

'But it must be exhausting, if you care about all the kids you meet.'

'You learn to manage it, but some cases hit home more than others.'

'Like Chaneth? I'm not asking you to break his confidence, but if I can help in any way I'd like to.'

'His story isn't a secret, but it is a traumatic one. His parents were criminals, caught up in gang warfare. Chaneth was brought up to follow in their footsteps. Pickpocketing, drug running, the works. Then when he was four-teen his parents were gunned down. He took to the streets and ended up headed to prison. Edwina heard about his case, stepped in and brought him to the orphanage. But he says he doesn't know any other life, is convinced it is in his blood, that once he goes he'll go back to a life of crime. That his family will make him. He believes he can't fight his genes, his blood.'

'But that's not true.'

Matt shrugged. 'But it's what he feels, Zoe. The pull of the life he knows, the tug of family, the knowledge that his parents did bad things.' His voice was grim, his eyes were shadowed and she sensed how much he cared for this young man's plight. 'I took him to a boxing gym and he exhausted himself. But that's not a long-term solution.'

'It's all so sad,' she said fiercely. 'So many of their stories are tragic.'

'Yes. But that doesn't mean they need pity.'

She glanced at him. 'There is a difference between pity and sympathy.'

'I know that, but it's a fine line. Those children need practical help—Chaneth needs a home and a job.'

'They need emotional help too.'

'I know. Chaneth punched a bag harder than I've ever seen anyone hit anything. After that we talked.' He raised a hand. 'I realise that's not enough. I'm going to look into finding a counsellor.'

Zoe hesitated. 'Did you ever have counselling?' she asked. 'After your parents died?'

'No. The social workers tried but I wasn't

receptive. I accept and believe counselling is effective and useful…'

'But not for you?'

'Not for me.' He smiled. 'I managed fine without it.'

'It must have been awful though. I was speaking to Nimali. She told me about her background—she actually came from a fairly wealthy family and her parents sounded amazing. Loving, kind and wanted the best for her. But they died in a flood when Nimali was seven. She had no family willing to take her in and so she ended up in the orphanage.' Zoe shook her head. 'She is so brave; she told me, though, that what helps her are memories of her parents. She knows she was loved and she can still talk to them, even if she has to imagine their answers. It made me think of you—I guess it does help to have good memories.'

'Yes.' His voice was oddly colourless. 'I think it also helps that the orphanage offers the chance of moving into an extended family. The care system in the UK doesn't work like that. They place individual children into families who are paid to foster them. The problem with that for a child is he feels he's there because he is a job, and that however much the foster family appears to care for him, and may really care for him, he's a commodity. Or at least I did. It's a cost-benefit thing—is the child worth the money you're being paid?'

'That's horrible.' Zoe's heart ached at the thought of the serious dark-haired little boy estimating his own value.

'Yes and no. At the end of the day the system ensures you have a roof over your head and are fed and watered. And its aim is to make you feel part of the family, but that doesn't really work, because obviously you aren't. One of my families was great—I was there four years, but then the woman's mum got ill and needed to come to live with them. They needed my room so that was that. I was moved on. That won't happen to Nimali and I'm glad of that, because you can see how close they all are and how they look out for each other.' He leant back, rested on his arms as he looked out to sea. 'Perhaps I should also think of a way for them to stay in touch.'

'You could build or rent homes—they could move into them when they were eighteen, maybe flatshare. They would still need to pay rent and bills, but they could learn slowly rather than be catapulted to independence. Then those who wanted to stay local and stay in touch could do so more easily. It could be like a two-year transitional thing.'

He sat up straighter and looked directly into her eyes. 'That is an excellent idea. You do really care.'

'Yes. I do. I didn't expect to—I mean, I never once felt like this about any of my parents' causes. Maybe because they felt so abstract. This is real—I've seen it, met the people and I want to make a difference to their lives. My parents never made anything personal—they are activists. They organise marches, write letters, protest, and I get that that all has a place and is important, but it never fired me up.' She leant forward in the dusk. 'So I'm sorry if I ever was negative about your foundation or your cause. You are making a massive difference, not just here, but in all the work you do. Nimali told me that she hoped to make her parents proud of her. I know your parents would have been proud of you.'

The reaction was instant and unmistakeable.

The light in his eyes snuffed out and his gaze shadowed, and she could feel the tension stiffen his body; his lips twisted into a grimace and now palpable anger etched his features.

'I'm sorry.' Damn it. The man had made it clear he didn't want to discuss his parents;

it was clearly a grief he kept close to himself and didn't want to air. He'd barely mentioned them during their marriage and earlier he'd closed down rather than speak of them. 'I didn't mean to bring back painful memories. I just wanted to show you what an amazing job you are doing, what a difference you are making. But I shouldn't have brought your parents into it. I can't imagine how much you would have grieved and…' Oh, God. Why couldn't she shut up?

'I didn't grieve.' He sounded as if the words were torn out of him.

'I don't understand.' She shifted on the sand so she could see him more clearly, the pain on his face more jagged now. 'You don't have to tell me if you don't want to.'

'I do have to tell you, because hearing you speak of them as though they were good people who cared about me is wrong. They weren't. In truth I don't know if they are alive or dead or rotting in prison.'

A chill ran through her and she reached out and covered his hand, unsure if he even noticed the touch.

'They weren't good parents. They weren't good people. When social services intervened I was half-starved, dirty, and I could barely speak—I was five years old. I don't really remember those years. My parents are hazy figures, the sound of a rough voice, the smell of cigarette smoke, a hazy, fuzzy outline. From what I can gather I survived mostly because of other people. Friends or neighbours who would see me hanging around and give me scraps, and I think I used to scavenge in bins. So, no, my parents weren't people I wish to remember and I certainly don't want them to be proud of me.'

Zoe blinked back tears fiercely, knew how little Matt would appreciate them, knew he would see it simply as pity. And what she felt was compassion along with a molten jolt of fury at the thought of his parents.

'I am beyond sorry for what you went through. There are no words that can encompass the anger I feel towards your parents and I know that my anger must be a drop in the ocean compared to your own. But...' She shifted forward now, looked directly at him, took in the dark hair lit by moonlight, the cragginess of his features, the jut of his jaw, saw the shadows in his eyes. Reaching up, she cupped his jaw. The stubble made her skin tingle and for some reason made her want to cry. 'You...you are amazing. I am filled with such admiration for you. For that five-year-old who somehow negotiated that terrible beginning and foster care.' Her voice wobbled. 'I don't know how you came to terms with it all, but you did and then you grew into a good, caring person who helps others. So you should be proud of you.'

She shifted forward and, oh, so lightly brushed her lips across his, felt the shiver that ran through them both and then he shifted backwards.

She narrowed her eyes, knew what he was thinking. 'That wasn't a pity kiss, Matt Sutherland. It was a kiss of sheer desire for a man who I admire and fancy the pants off. It was a kiss to say thank you for sharing that with me. A kiss to say you are absolutely incredible. Got it?'

For a moment he simply glowered at her and then a small reluctant smile tipped his lips up. 'Got it.'

She rose to her feet, knew it was important now to keep things light, instinctively knew he wouldn't want an in-depth discussion of what he'd shared. 'So how does that omelette sound now? We can eat and talk about the next few days.'

'Sounds like a plan.'

'Good. I'm excited about the festival in Burati—it sounds beyond amazing. And so does the train journey.'

CHAPTER TEN

ZOE WAS RIGHT, Matt reflected the next day as they boarded the bright blue train that would take them to Burati. The open carriages were busy but not too busy and he saw food vendors climb aboard alongside them holding trays of food that made his mouth water and lit Zoe's eyes with interest.

No doubt in his mind that she would somehow find a way to communicate with at least one vendor and get a recipe for the street food on offer.

Warmth trickled over his chest and he knew the smile on his face would hold a hint of goofiness, but somehow the previous day had lightened him in some way. Sharing the truth about his parents had made him feel… lighter. *Careful, Matt.* Light was good, but he didn't need to get carried away towards goofiness. He and Zoe had trod that path, he'd let her in and in the end she'd left, moved on. Proving the dangers of getting involved, forming connections. They never lasted, just as none of his foster placements had. This time with Zoe was finite and he'd better not forget it.

But that didn't mean he couldn't enjoy her company for the next few days. Zoe looked round the train. 'This is so cool. I looked it up and we can even stand in the open doorways if we're careful. And the views are meant to be incredible.'

They absolutely were. As the journey continued they sat and watched, mesmerised by the scenery that sometimes flashed by the window or more often sauntered past as the train wound its way across the tracks. The landscape segued and morphed, the scent of the tea plantations wafting in through the windows an almost heady aroma as they saw the women in brightly coloured saris tend the fields, the sunlight glinting off the crops. Then from tea they moved to mountains and rolling hills shrouded in mist, villages where children played, then in a blink of an eye woodlands zipped past the windows.

But if he was a hundred per cent honest, despite the undeniable beauty of the landscape he found his gaze flicking to Zoe. Dressed simply in cropped trousers and a sleeveless vest top, she looked fresh, cool and ridiculously pretty. He recalled last night, the brush of her lips against his, and desire jolted through him.

It was a relief to see the food vendor enter the carriage and he grinned as Zoe turned and rose to approach him, watched the dialogue conducted mostly in gestures as she purchased a selection of the aromatic snacks and brought them over to him.

'I have no real idea what these are but they smell incredible. So I need you to taste them and try and figure out what's in them. I think this is a *vadai*—it's like a savoury doughnut made of lentils—and then these are mini samosas, and I'm not sure what this is—a kind of roll. Imagine if... No, imagine *when* I can make these. They will make the most amazing starters or shared platter as a dish.'

Matt took a bite and closed his eyes. 'Definitely cumin and chilli and maybe a hint of lime,' he stated.

Zoe picked one up and tasted it. 'Maybe a pinch of fennel as well.'

Again his gaze lingered on her, the lushness of her lips, the look of intense concentration as she savoured the food.

'What? Sorry, have I got crumbs all over me?' she asked.

'No. I was just thinking I'm glad we did this. Accepted David and Manisha's gift.' Though once again he wondered what David's motives had been.

'Me too.'

Now there was a silence, almost as if they were cocooned from the sounds of the other passengers, the whoosh of the breeze through the windows. Their gazes meshed and Matt couldn't help it—he smiled. 'Me too, too.'

Her answering smile lit her face. 'Good. I'm glad.' She took a deep breath. 'Over the next few days shall we try to enjoy ourselves? It is such good news that David's op went well, and the prognosis is good, and this is such a beautiful place to be… I don't want to have to keep worrying about giving out the wrong signals. We both know this can't go anywhere, whatever this is between us, so let's just relax.'

For a fraction of a moment he hesitated. The words made sense, he did know this could go nowhere, but that knowledge was fighting against a hope that somehow it could. A misguided hope that he had to shut down. And the best way to do that would be to call a halt now; he should get off at the next platform and take the train back. But he couldn't. Not when he saw how relaxed Zoe looked, the spark in her eye, the anticipation. It would be OK—it was only three days; he'd take care... 'Suits me.' Yet a sense of disquiet remained for the rest of the journey to Burati, the beautiful city nestled in the hills of Sri Lanka.

They alighted from the train and looked around the bustling station, the noise and colour and sheer vibrancy of the city as immediate as the blast of heat. The mingle of scents, the clamour of voices interspersed with the hubbub of birds.

'I love it already,' Zoe said. 'Do you think we can walk to our hotel?'

'There should be a tuk-tuk waiting for us.'

Sure enough, they spotted a man holding a placard with their names on it. Matt waved and they headed over to the three-wheeled, open-door vehicle and climbed aboard, absorbing their surroundings as the taxi weaved its way through the busy streets, horn at the ready.

Colonial architecture mixed with brightly coloured buildings, street markets flourished in a random arrangement throughout and above the city the hills and mountains loomed and rolled as the pungent scent from the tea and spice plantations added to the culture and feel of the city.

A few minutes and the tuk-tuk screeched

to a stop at their destination, a low-roofed sprawl of a hotel. The stone-clad building was shaded by enormous fronded palm trees and surrounded by a lush tropical garden, beautifully landscaped into a riot of verdant greens and rich exotic colours that lit the whole area up.

They thanked the driver and Matt followed Zoe into the welcome cool of the hotel. Cool marble floors and slate-grey walls housed a sweep of a reception desk tempered by wicker chairs and low tables, the overall effect the perfect medley of comfort and modernity.

'Welcome,' a smiling staff member said. 'We have put you in the top-floor suite. Due to the festival it isn't possible to put you in separate rooms, but we have put an additional bed in the lounge area of the suite—I hope that is acceptable.'

A heartbeat and then Zoe nodded. 'Absolutely.' What else could she say? Matt realised. The thought of finding another hotel was daunting.

'Then let me show you to your suite. You will be going out for the festival processions today?'

'Definitely. We can't wait.'

Zoe halted on the threshold of the suite and

turned to Matt, her mouth forming a small O of appreciation. 'This is incredible.'

Once the woman had left she turned to Matt. 'I feel bad that Dylan and Beth are missing out on this. I'm sure in different circumstances David would have wanted them to come here.'

'I am sure they will come back. In fact I will insist they do even if I have to book their tickets.'

'Ooh. Maybe we should do that and we can give it to them as a gift after their reception.'

'It's a plan.' A small niggle warned him that he shouldn't be making future plans with Zoe, however innocuous. Told him that he was getting carried away by the décor, the sheer romantic opulence of the surroundings. Which was ridiculous—Matt Sutherland was not a romantic man. Yet as he looked round the room and his gaze fell on the enormous four-poster bed, replete with pillows and cushions, surrounded by the fluttering lace of a gauzy curtain, when he saw the tall vases filled with arrangements of greens and browns, the floating candles, inhaled the cocktail of scents from the open window, it became increasingly difficult to heed the voice of common sense.

Especially when he looked at Zoe, took in her beauty and grace and the sheer rightness of her being here. He blinked, aware that she had said something.

'Sorry?'

'I said I hope it's OK, the idea of us sharing the suite, and also I'll have the spare bed.'

'No, I'll have the spare bed. It makes no difference to me.'

'Well, it makes a difference to me.' She jutted her chin out. 'From what you told me yesterday you spent a lot of your life being given the worst bedroom in the house, so not today. Today you get that bed there and that's final.'

'But that's—'

'What's going to happen. So let's not waste time arguing. I'm going to change and then we need to go. I want to make sure we see as much of the procession as possible, and I want to soak up all the festival atmosphere.'

'Sounds like a plan.' Another one, he realised, even as warmth trickled into his chest at her gesture.

Another tuk-tuk ride later and Zoe looked round the city centre in sheer awe; the vibe from the city was one of exuberance and noise and business and without even consulting she took Matt's hand in hers, knowing how easy it would be to be swept away.

'I don't know where to look first,' she said.

'It's all so incredible…full of life and joy. And I get why—this is the most important festival of the year and incredibly meaningful. A time when the most sacred of—' She broke off.

'Tell me,' he said.

She glanced at him. 'But I bet you already know.'

He shrugged. 'Doesn't matter. It becomes more alive when you tell it.'

'OK. This is the time when the most sacred of relics is carried through the streets, a relic that is usually guarded as being beyond precious in a temple named after it. This relic is said to have belonged to Buddha himself and it used to be that the person who owned it wielded the power to rule the island.' Her eyes were wide. 'Can you imagine that? The wars that must have been fought and the blood shed over it, even though it is meant to be holy and spiritual and surely a thing of peace.'

'Many powerful rulers believed they fought in order to bring peace to their land.' He shook his head. 'I'm glad that now this relic only brings awe and worship and joy.'

'Look how quiet it is now.' An expectant hush had fallen on the crowds and then the boom of a cannon burst onto the evening air, followed by the raucous cries of celebration from the crowd at the knowledge the procession was under way.

'Look.' Zoe pointed at a group of dancers. They were dressed in a swirl of red, their movements incredibly fast and perfectly synchronised as somehow they weaved their way through the packed streets of people. The sound of drums beat through the air, accompanied by the chant of the crowds.

And then they saw the golden torchlight in the distance, and the noise from the streets died down a little as the procession came closer and closer, heralded by men dressed in glorious vibrant blues and golds, brandishing whips that whipped the air with a crack of noise and twisted and curved in spirals of sound. Now she could see the turbaned drummers, drums hanging around their necks as they marched, followed by flag bearers.

Music strummed the air and she gazed in wonder at the robed musicians whose chants carried through the breeze, the sound both serious and light, full of joy and awe. As for the acrobats, Zoe knew she would never forget the tumble and roll, the cartwheels, the sheer exotic exuberance, all lit by the almost mystical torchlight.

Then the priests walked past, and she squeezed Matt's hand as a line of richly adorned elephants lumbered by, their broad backs swathed in gorgeous cloths of gold and red.

Once past, the rhythm of the crowd tugged them in their wake and for a while they followed until Matt pointed to the side of the road, where street vendors plied their trade. 'There will be plenty more to see,' he said. 'But first shall we get something to eat?'

So they ate *ulundu vadai*, spicy lentil doughnuts, and *kottu roti*, salty spiced pieces of fried dough, cooked with a selection of vegetables. Zoe watched with delight as the vendor rhythmically chopped the *roti*, singing in time to the clank of his knife and the beat of his spatula as he cooked. Then she turned to marvel at the array of dancers, musicians and singers that followed in the wake of the official procession, and the most glittering troupe of fire dancers, who lit the night air with a magical display of lights that orbed and circled in time with them.

'I'll never forget this,' Zoe said.

'Neither will I,' Matt said softly. 'It's been a truly magical night.'

She looked up at him. 'I don't want the magic to end.' She gave a sudden shaky laugh, knew the magic hadn't been just in the sights, however amazing they were. It was the company, the knowledge that Matt had shared her wonder, the way he'd looked as he saw the elephants go by, his appreciation of what was behind this festival, the history and the significance. 'I feel a bit like the relic. Allowed out for a while but knowing that I'll end up locked back up because that is the safest thing to do. I don't feel like being safe today. I want to…' And in that moment she knew exactly what she wanted to do, needed to do. 'Do this.' With that she turned, already so close to him that all she had to do was stand on tiptoe and wrap her arms round his neck, felt his arms loop her waist and then in one sinuous movement they meshed together, his lips on hers. Her head spun, swam with dizzy relief and a sense of utter gloriousness.

The sounds of the festival faded into the background, the stars and the torchlight illuminating the backdrop for a kiss that seemed timeless and infinite. Her whole body was completely under the spell of the havoc his lips created; sensations vortexed through her as she tasted him. The spice, the hint of chilli, the texture of his hair under her fingers, the brand of his fingers through the thin silk of her dress.

Finally they pulled apart and stared at each other wide-eyed.

'Come on,' he said. 'Let's walk.' He smiled at her, a slow smile that sent a thrill shivering through her. 'Let's eat, let's sample food and drink and the sights of this city. Together. And then…'

'Then…?' she asked.

'Let's see what happens.'

Oh, so gently, he reached out, tucked a tendril of hair behind her ear, and now her shiver must be visible as she gazed at him, lips parted, and saw desire darken his eyes to cobalt.

'Sounds like a plan,' she said and, reaching up, she cupped his jaw. 'But whatever happens I will never regret that kiss or forget this evening.'

As they walked, Zoe lost herself in the moment, in her surroundings, delighted in the illuminated outsides of the temples, and the sheer aura of the city. 'It's such an amazing place, so steeped in history, I can almost see the different eras fuzz in the air today. As though there are layers of the past.' She went silent and then, 'I suppose that's what builds the present, isn't it? Layers of the past.'

'Yes, but it is the present that's important, isn't it? If we focused on the past we'd get caught in those layers and they wouldn't let us go. So the key is to build new layers so each present layer is a good one building towards a better future.' Matt grinned. 'Hey, this is getting a bit deep, isn't it?' He looked round. 'How about we take an evening hike? I'm pretty sure I read about a viewpoint where you can look down over the city by night.'

'That sounds lovely.' It did, but Zoe suspected the reason for the suggestion was two-fold. It stopped a conversation that dwelled on the past. After all, neither she nor Matt had much use for the past. Now she understood his desire to run from those original layers, to build as many new ones as possible to separate him from the horror of his start in life.

As for herself. She'd been running one way or the other all her life. Running from her parents to gain attention, then running from the past ever since the moment she'd heard of Tom's death. Even her marriage to Matt had been a way of escape from the tragedy and guilt. A chance to atone. But each experience, each layer, each new recipe learnt, each new job, new country, built a new layer and that was good, right?

Definitely heading into deep philosophical waters. She glanced at Matt, wondered what he was thinking as their steps took them further away from the chaotic bustle of the city towards the outskirts, where revellers still danced and laughter and happiness mingled in the air.

She knew too that his suggestion for a walk was to put off a decision as to what happened next after that kiss. A kiss that still reverberated through her, her lips tingling, her whole body in a state of heightened sensory perception. The lights seemed brighter, the scents of food stronger, her own body felt buoyant as they walked together, even the steepness of the hill didn't faze her, as they wound their way upwards along the dusty road.

But she knew the right thing to do, the sensible thing to do, was walk and walk, walk away the pent-up attraction in each step, march up the hill until tiredness, exhaustion, muted the yearn to take things further. Because last time they had let heady attraction carry them away it had carried them both to pain and misery. Matt was not her Mr Right. Zoe quickened her pace, felt the ache in her calf muscles as they overtook the few other people also wending their way upwards.

They reached the summit and Zoe gazed downward in sheer awe at the panoramic vista spread below them. The deep blue night sky spread like a cloak to the horizon, patterned with lush green forest, the perfect backdrop to the city below, illuminated with golden flashing lights, the distant buildings shapes of blazing colour.

'It's beautiful,' she said. 'I guess, though, that a city has layers too. I mean, years ago people standing here would have seen a completely different scene. Centuries ago there would have been nothing—the trees and forest wouldn't even have been saplings. Then slowly over those centuries people would have started to build. The first temple maybe five hundred years ago, slowly going up, a place of worship. At another point of time standing here we may have seen bloodshed and battles as people fought for the right to rule this place. In another we would have seen the growth of the city, colonial buildings going up alongside the original architecture.'

'All things that bring us to the here and now. You and me standing here, looking over a place of peace and prosperity.'

You and me. The words seemed to take on a significance as they hovered in the air. This moment was one she knew she would remember for ever: a time of understanding and closeness, a time where a decision hung in the balance.

Zoe stared out at the vista, searched her heart and mind. What did she want? The answer was obvious. She wanted Matt. But

she knew too that she couldn't have him—
he wasn't her Mr Right, wasn't the man who
could give her what she truly wanted. So a
future with Matt wasn't possible. It never had
been. Years ago, if she hadn't fallen pregnant,
she would have worked that out—once she'd
realised he didn't want a family.

So a future was an impossibility. Fact. But
the attraction existed, the chemistry, the need,
were undeniable. Fact. And she wanted to
act on it.

'Matt?' The word was a question and a
whisper.

He turned, his face serious in the starlight,
a question in his eyes.

'About you and me. About the past and
the future. Here and now we're in between.
I know we don't have a future, but we do
have here and now, and I'd like to…make it
count. For it to become a layer in my life.' She
shrugged. 'I get that sounds absurd.'

His turn now to look away out into the
night's vista as he thought and then he turned
back. 'It doesn't sound absurd.' He gave a half
laugh, though it held rue rather than mirth.
'Though I suspect it probably is absurd. But
I'm not sure how we'd make it work.' She
studied his expression, wondered if this was
a diplomatic rejection, saw that it wasn't. His

eyes held desire and a genuine question. As if he sensed her thoughts, he took her hand in his. 'I'm open to ideas—I just know we can't...'

'Afford to repeat history. I know.' Her fingers tightened round his. 'And we won't. We can't. This time round we both know what we want from life, and we know we can't give it to each other long-term. But maybe we can have something in the here and now, take something out of your relationship manual. Short-term and fun.'

'Take the chance to have what it is possible for us to have.' There was a hint of sadness in his voice and instinctively she got it. So much of his life must have felt like that— life with a good foster family for as long as it was possible for him to have it. As if he realised it himself, he gave a small shake of his head as if to abandon negativity. 'Are you sure about this, Zoe? That this is what you want. Because we will still need to see each other in the future.'

He was right, but... 'I know, but maybe the knowledge that we did this, had this layer, will mean we know it's finished business. This time we've got boundaries.' She thought for a moment. 'What if we put a time limit on it? We have fun whilst we are in Sri Lanka.

Let's stay on in Burati for the whole festival. I am pretty sure that will take us up to the time when David will be well enough to travel again. So that's when we do what you said. Resume normal life at the end of our relationship. Our shallow relationship,' she added hurriedly. 'What do you think?'

His face was inscrutable, and she wished she could access the whir of his brain. And then he smiled, a smile that curled her toes. 'I would be honoured to paddle in the shallow end with you.'

Now she smiled, slow and languorous. 'I think you said something about recharging batteries? And there was the offer of fun. In and out of bed.'

'Which type of fun would you like first?'

'Right now? I think we should get a tuk-tuk back to the hotel and I'll show you.' She grinned at him. 'And, even better, we get to share the four-poster.'

CHAPTER ELEVEN

MATT WOKE UP with a deep sense of well-being, opened his eyes and made sure to keep his body still and relaxed so as not to wake Zoe up. She lay curled in the crook of his arm, her luscious hair tickling his chest, one slim leg wrapped around his.

The sensations were so new and yet so familiar, and the deep sense of contentment triggered a sudden sense of doubt. Had they made the right decision? Had this been a foolish premise, to believe he and Zoe could safely navigate any sort of relationship? It would be fine, he told himself. Hell, he was the best risk assessor in the business—he could read the market, use instincts and statistics to figure out where to place millions, to play the odds to maximise profit.

And he would not listen to the small voice that warned him this was foolish. They were making a layer, that was all, a single layer, a sliver of time. It made no difference if it were three days or ten. At the end they would resume normal life—he *knew* how to do this. This would work—because this time round there was no commitment, no prospect of having to be a family man, no chance he could let Zoe down in any way. So there was no risk. No need for emotions to become messy or complicated.

Plus, it was simply impossible to believe the previous night had been a mistake. As he gazed up at the stark white of the ceiling the events seemed to play out like a movie. The tuk-tuk ride had been carried out in a silence that had shivered with fevered anticipation and, as if he'd sensed it, the driver had hurtled down the road and through the still-busy streets at hair-raising speed.

Once back at the hotel there had still been no need for words. They'd raced up the stairs, almost indecent in their haste, Zoe's breathless laugh as they'd near on collided in the doorway. He'd intended finesse, slowness, but instead there had been frenzied greed, their fingers fumbling with buttons, the desperate need to touch almost too much.

And then they'd tumbled onto the four-poster bed, onto the silken sheets, finally able to assuage the yearning, to feel, to touch, her hands sweeping down his back, as he kissed the sweet spot on her neck, both of them carried away on a tide of exquisite pleasure and a wave of deep release.

As if sensing the direction of his thoughts as his body reacted to remembered pleasure, Zoe moved against him, lifted her head and surveyed him with sleep-filled eyes.

'Morning,' he said.

'Morning,' she replied, and looked at him slightly speculatively. 'Wow. Did we really…?'

'Yup, we really did. Everything you remember and possibly more. Definitely not a dream,' he said, unable to keep the slightly smug look from his face. 'Definitely as good as you remember it.'

Her gurgle of laughter as she thumped him gently on the chest made him smile back in return. 'Oh, really?' she said.

'Absolutely really.'

'Then why don't you prove it?' And in one lithe movement she straddled him, looked down at him with pure provocation in her eyes, a provocation that morphed to desire as his smile widened.

'Gladly,' he growled.

Half an hour later she laid her head on his shoulder, as they sat up and leant back against the mahogany headboard, sated, sheet tangled around their legs, thigh to thigh, hand in hand. 'You win. That was definitely as good as I remembered.'

'I think we both won,' he said, and she grinned.

'No arguments here.'

She shifted slightly so she could look at him. 'So what shall we do today?'

He wiggled his eyebrows. 'I have an idea. But you may need to give me, say...half an hour.'

She grinned at him. 'That is not what I meant! I thought we could go and visit the temple where the relic is held? I'd like to go and send positive vibes to David in a place of worship.'

'I like that idea.'

'But I'm willing to wait half an hour and then go.'

'Sounds like a plan.'

A few hours later, Zoe gazed up at the temple complex surrounded by a moat. The buildings were simpler than she had expected with white stone walls and red roofs. The whole had an almost layered effect, and she tried not to read anything into the thought. *Get a grip.* The temple had been built centuries before—it certainly hadn't been designed to accommodate her metaphorical view of time.

She studied the walls, saw the carved apertures that housed lamps and candles. 'Those must have been some of the lights we saw last night from the viewpoint,' she said to Matt, and he nodded as they moved forward in the queue.

Zoe had read the guidelines and made sure she was wearing a long flowing sundress, with a high neck and short sleeves, and she had covered the whole with a light cardigan. The very last thing she wanted to do was show any disrespect—especially as she knew this was a genuine place of worship and that many inside would be there, not as tourists, but to pray.

Both she and Matt slipped their shoes off at the entrance and then entered the temple. 'Wow,' she breathed, and after that by tacit consent neither spoke, and she felt a sudden warmth at his instinctive understanding, that they were on the same page, knew this was a place they were privileged to be allowed into.

An impression that grew as they made their way through the interior. Because whilst she couldn't help but admire the intricate beauty on display, the bright red of the ceilings, the marbled white of the walls, the mosaic floors and the abundance of detailed carvings, what was most obvious was the sense of serenity imbued by the obvious devotion of the locals who placed their offerings of flowers at the shrine where the relic was housed. As she walked, Zoe allowed the worries about Matt and if she was doing the right thing to ebb away, focused instead on all she had to be thankful for, hoped and prayed that David would be all right.

By the time they left, retrieved their shoes and started walking, Zoe had slipped her hand into Matt's, revelling in the fact she was allowed to do so. 'Part of me feels as though we shouldn't have gone in there as tourists, that we shouldn't be watching people communing, praying, worshipping. But part of me feels really grateful they did let us in because it's clearly such a sacred place and somehow that's given me a sense of peace.'

Matt nodded. 'I know what you mean. Faith is a wonderful thing and here in this place it is authentic and clearly provides comfort and peace.'

Zoe considered his words. 'Do you think the kids at the orphanage go to temple?' she asked. 'Or church? Or do you think they've lost their faith because of what happened to them?'

Matt looked arrested. 'I don't know,' he said. 'But it's something I'll ask. See if that is something we can provide more access to—a spiritual person. Not to convert them, but perhaps to find out about that aspect of their backgrounds.' He squeezed her hand. 'Where to now? I was thinking you may want to sample some restaurants, get some ideas? So we could map out a selection. I did find one near here that we could start with. I asked one of the hotel staff, a groundsman. He says his parents own it and it's the real thing.'

'That sounds perfect.' Too perfect. Irrationally she wanted to ask him not to be so thoughtful. *Ridiculous.* Thoughtful was good and liking Matt was fine. Presumably you couldn't have a shallow relationship with someone you didn't like. The key was to remember Matt was being thoughtful and kind and relaxed *because* this was a shallow, fun relationship. Just as he'd been before she'd fallen pregnant and they'd got married. After that, yes, he'd been thoughtful in that he'd worked his butt off to provide, but he hadn't been relaxed. He'd pulled away from her because he didn't want a family or commitment. So however thoughtful he was, he was not Mr Right. But that didn't mean she couldn't enjoy the moment. The here and now.

It was a mantra she stuck to over the next days, days that passed in a haze of food and drink and sightseeing and nights filled with magic and joy. They toured the botanical gardens, visited a tea plantation and took evening walks around the central lake. And, of course, continued their tour of restaurants, spent ages researching and planning.

'I've got high hopes of this one,' Zoe said on day four of their stay as they wandered the now familiar streets, chatting or silent as the mood took them until they reached the small restaurant tucked into a meandering alleyway, crowded with a market that seemed to have sprung up from nowhere.

The restaurant itself was filled with locals and brightly lit, the inside held square plastic tables and the aroma that wafted out made Zoe pause and simply inhale in sheer appreciation.

'Lead on,' she said, and soon they were tucked into a tiny table looking down at an all-vegetarian menu. A waiter headed towards them and Zoe beamed at him. 'I'd like to have the *masala dosa*. I've had them in India but never here.'

'Ours are much better,' he said promptly. 'Here we use more *dal* and less rice in the batter and you will love our filling, though it is spicy. It also comes with coconut chutney and various sauces.'

'Perfect.'

'I'll have the *thali* and the potato *bonda*,' Matt said. He smiled at her after the waiter had gone. 'And you're welcome to try all of it—that way you'll get a wide-ranging sample.'

Zoe smiled at him. 'Thank you. Really. The *bonda* sounds yummy and you can obviously have some of my *dosa*. If you can take the spice,' she added with a teasing grin that called an answering one from him.

'As long as it's not like that curry we had on our third date.'

Zoe gurgled with laughter. 'I don't think I'll ever forget your face when you tasted it.' They had been discussing hot food and Matt had decided to try the hottest thing on the menu, a vegetarian phall.

'The worst thing was that there was a part of me thinking I should tough it out, be macho, and a sane part of me pointing out that at worst I'd die, at best I'd turn bright red and run round the restaurant with flames coming out of my mouth.' He sipped his beer and laughed. 'Thank goodness you came up with a solution.'

'Yup. I suggested we ask them to package it up and we could use it as a condiment. Not that we ever did.'

'Well, if any of the curries here are of a

similar heat I'll know what to do.' He leant back slightly. 'On a serious note, though, what will you do if you open a restaurant in the UK? I mean, it is possible that the heat levels that are authentic will be too much for the British palate. You hear a lot about Asian restaurants having to trade in authenticity for realism and profit.'

She nodded. 'Of course. There is no point providing authentic food that will actually cause discomfort to your customers, or that no one will eat. I think the answer is to be honest. On the menu you say you have kept it as "real" as possible, but you've dialled down the chilli side of it. And maybe have different grade levels and I also thought, based on our experience, perhaps you provide authentic taster cups—so customers can have the tiniest taste of why I've dialled it down.' She paused for breath. 'Or I decide to appeal to a niche audience of people who really like hot food and I make my restaurant based on authentic hot food, or I have hot food on the menu. But obviously I'm not Sri Lankan or Indian so, again, I need to be honest. I kind of want it to be themed with the idea of food from my travels…' She paused again as the waiter arrived with their food. 'Sorry, I'll stop burbling on.'

'You aren't burbling at all. I'm interested.'

She popped a piece of *dosa* into her mouth and closed her eyes to savour the taste. 'This is incredible.' She sighed suddenly. 'And maybe I could create a *masala dosa* as good as this with my own spin—but I know starting a restaurant is so much more than being able to cook.' She looked at him. 'However good a cook I am, it takes more, and I know that. Just like, presumably, however good you are at investing, that's not enough to set up your own business.'

'No. I made sure I had plenty of capital saved. I also had a pretty good reputation and I started small. A few select clients. Also good publicity. And a plan—short-, medium- and long-term goals.'

She nodded. 'I thought I'd set up small— travel round the UK to various festivals and street markets—whilst I'm also working a paid job.'

'Also use social media. If you can gather a large following, or catch the eye of a prominent food critic, or get enough local interest so that a national paper interviews you, that will make a massive difference. I'd start right now—start a food blog, get yourself on You-Tube.' He smiled at her. 'What about a long-term goal?'

'If I'm dreaming big I'd like to own at least three restaurants. I'd like a Michelin star. I'd like to write a bestseller cookbook. In reality, though, I would be really happy with one established, profitable restaurant that gave me job fulfilment and security to support my family.' *Family.* The word brought a sudden awkwardness to the flow of conversation, a blip.

'Perhaps your Mr Right will be in the restaurant business,' he said, and she looked at him. At first glance there was nothing but ease in his stance or expression, but she could see the slight set to his jaw and a shade of rigidity to his shoulders.

And as she studied him further it became harder and harder to even picture the fuzziest image of any 'Mr Right'. *Enough.* This was all about attraction and liking each other. That did not make Mr Right. A thrill of caution ran through her, a sudden temptation to up and run, a fear that she was getting pulled in almost without realising it. So perhaps now was a good time to focus on her future just for a while. A reminder that this was a temporary bubble on her way to her dream, a single finite layer of her life.

'Perhaps,' she said. 'But I'd rather he wasn't.'

'Why?'

'Because we would be too interdependent. I need to know that, if it comes to it, I can support my children by myself. And there is also a chance that Mr Right won't materialise. In which case I'll be having children on my own. So I need my business to be mine and I need it to generate enough income to provide my kids with a good life.' As she thought about the idea of children, the ship steadied for a moment. A small boy, dark hair mussed and spiky, brown eyes and a wide gummy smile, a replica of...of Matt.

Oh, hell and damnation.

This had to stop. Matt did not want children; there would be no mini Matts. Now she scrunched her eyes closed, determinedly conjured up a red-haired little girl and a blond boy, both of them with green eyes. That was better, much better.

'And I want to be there for my kids. So if that means toning down my business dreams in favour of my family, that's good with me. I will not miss a single important moment—I want to be there for their first smile, first tooth, first step...'

He gave an almost imperceptible flinch and she broke off, wanted to kick herself round the restaurant and out on the street. Because Matt's parents hadn't given a damn about his first anything, hadn't cared enough to even give him enough food or clothes and that must hurt. But his gaze met hers and she knew that he would take any apology as pity, a pity that he would take as an insult.

'That is as it should be,' he said evenly. 'You will be a wonderful mother, Zoe.' He lifted his glass. 'To your future.'

'Thank you.' Yet even as she raised her glass, that dark-haired little boy flitted across her mind. She forced a smile to her face. 'But enough talk of the future.' After all, they only had a few days left before that future would be reality. 'This is meant to be about the present and the here and now.'

'The here and now,' he echoed, but she was sure she could see a strain behind his smile.

CHAPTER TWELVE

THE FOLLOWING MORNING, Matt slid carefully out of bed, breath held so as not to wake Zoe, and headed for the bathroom. Once shaved, he surveyed himself in the mirror, almost surprised to see that he didn't look different.

Because he felt different, and the knowledge grated his nerves, the feelings a throwback to when he'd met Zoe the first time round. Back then he'd let his guard slip, let Zoe get under his skin and inspire feelings that he couldn't handle and that had ultimately led to pain and abandonment. The only other time he'd done that in his life had been with foster carers who he'd lived with for four years. When he'd heard they were moving him on he'd been devastated inside—only pride had allowed him to hold it together. Outwardly at least. That had been one of the times when he'd punched walls; he'd simply done it in private and hidden the damage.

He turned away from the mirror, knew it was time to pull back—the conversation the previous night had showed him that. Zoe had a future and he wouldn't forget it. That was why he'd arranged a surprise for her this morning, something that would help her future and hopefully she'd enjoy it.

Moving back to the bedroom, he glanced down at Zoe, took in the long eyelashes, the ripple of red hair, the curve of her body under the sheet, and there it was, that trickle of warmth, the stir of emotional connection. Leaning down, he shook her gently awake, smiled as she squinted up at him through sleep-filled eyes. 'You're up,' she said.

'Very observant.' Laughter filled his voice.

'But it's not even six.' She smiled at him. 'I think you should just come back to bed.'

'That is a very tempting idea, but I've got something planned for you.'

'You do? For me?'

'Yup, so come on. Up you get.'

She rubbed her eyes and sat up. 'OK. I'm curious so I'll play along.'

Fifteen minutes later she looked around from the seat of the tuk-tuk, studied the route with a small frown of concentration. 'We're going back to the *dosa* place,' she realised. 'Will it be open yet?'

'Nope. I've booked you a culinary lesson— the owner and chef is going to show you how he makes *dosa* and various fillings. I thought it would be useful, but also something you can use on social media and to promote your food at street markets and so on. Premandi, the owner, has agreed to get his daughter-in-law to video the whole thing as well.'

'That's...' Zoe blinked back tears and then moved closer to him and kissed him '...incredibly thoughtful. Thank you, Matt.'

'You're more than welcome,' he replied as they turned into the alleyway and saw the owner wave cheerfully to them from the restaurant door. 'Enjoy and I'll be back in a few hours.'

As he walked away guilt touched him— yes, he had done it for Zoe, but he knew too it was also a reminder to himself that this time with her was finite, and he hoped some time spent without her would give him time to process and make sure his guard was firmly in place. Yet as he walked the hustle and bustle of the streets, stopped for a coffee, he missed her, missed the feel of her hand in his, her pithy commentary or the way she sometimes just walked in silence. Missed the turn of her head, her scent, her... For Pete's sake. He quickened his pace in exasperation, felt re-lief when his phone rang.

A relief that was short-lived.

'Matt. It's Edwina. I am so sorry to trouble you but Prisha asked me to, begged me to, because she thought maybe you could help. I am not sure what you can do but I promised her so...'

Matt could hear the panic in Edwina's voice, knew he needed to figure out what was going on even as scenarios chased through his mind. 'Are the children OK?'

'Yes. For now. But...' Edwina's voice broke. 'Her husband has found her.' Matt's blood ran cold. His head swam as Edwina continued. 'He turned up here and tried to take her by force. Thank goodness Chaneth was in the kitchen with her. He grabbed a knife and he managed to get rid of him. They called me and I called the police. But now it turns out that the husband has a lawyer—he says he is legally entitled to the children, that he wants them back, and he is also filing charges against Chaneth and...'

The world seemed to fragment. It was as though the completely unexpected words had caught him unawares, his barriers down, and for a blinding moment the stuff of his night-mares became real. The fuzzy people he could never see clearly struggled to come into focus and this time he could hear the wail of a baby and the sound of rough, raised voices, yelling at it in profanities to shut up.

He closed the images down instantly. He couldn't afford to let them in. Not now.

'Edwina, listen to me. I'm on my way. In the meantime I'll get a couple of security guards to the orphanage and I'll get on to a lawyer. Do not let anyone take Prisha away and do not let those children out of your sight.'

He hung up and then dialled Zoe's number.

'It's Matt.' He briefly explained the situation. 'I'm arranging security and getting a lawyer and I'm sorry, Zoe, I'll need to go back.'

He had to. He couldn't, wouldn't, let those children or Prisha be handed back to a violent man. Would not put them at risk of injury or death. No more children would die on his watch. Which meant he had to be there. He wouldn't desert Chaneth either. The boy did not deserve to go to jail.

'I'm sorry,' he said again. Knew that to Zoe this would be a repeat of her parents' behaviour.

There wasn't even a pause before, 'What are you on about? Why are you sorry? I'm coming too—of course we are going back. We can't stay here having fun whilst Prisha and her babies are in danger.'

'Are you sure?'

'Of course I'm sure, and I'm horrified and insulted that you would even think I would do any different. On a practical note, I'll take over the kitchens—that way Prisha can focus on being with the children or seeing a lawyer. So if possible we need to stay at or near the orphanage. Anyway, we can discuss details later. I'll head back to the hotel and meet you there.'

Even in the grip of panic Matt felt a sense of warmth, an appreciation at Zoe's words, the instant offer of help with a pragmatism to back it up.

The next few hours were caught up in getting themselves from the city back to the orphanage as fast as possible whilst keeping in touch with Edwina.

As they sat in the hire car, he tried to relax. Logic told him they couldn't get there any quicker.

'Hey.' She reached out and put her hand on his leg; the contact gave comfort. 'You have done everything you can do. You've found a lawyer and the security has arrived and it's unlikely the husband will try anything violent now.'

'I wish he would. That way we'd have something against him.' He sighed. 'The lawyer is the best we can get but the problem is, how do we prove the man is violent? And what if he even wins visitation rights or custody? Once he gets his hands on those kids…'

Worry etched Zoe's face. 'I know, and I'm worried sick too. But at least we know right now they are all safe and I know you will do everything you can do to keep them that way. And Chaneth as well.'

Damn right he would. 'I'll feel better when we get there.'

And eventually the car pulled to a stop outside the orphanage and within minutes they were inside. Matt watched as Zoe engulfed Prisha in a hug. 'I am so sorry.'

The young woman shook her head, her face pale. 'He…he said he wouldn't rest until he had us back. That the kids are his, that I deserve to be punished for depriving my kids of a father. I was so scared. And Tomas, he hasn't spoken since. He is asleep now. What am I going to do? And poor Chaneth… But if he hadn't been there…'

Hearing her panic, he knew what he needed to do, would not let even a hint of his own agitation emerge. 'Prisha, listen to me. I will not let anyone hurt a hair on your children's heads, certainly not a man who does not deserve the title of father. Or husband. You are safe. I will fix this.' And he would—he would do whatever it took, no matter what. 'You focus on Tomas and Adam.'

Tomas made a small noise, a whimper, and instantly she moved to his side.

Matt watched as the young woman carefully took the baby out of the sling and put him into the small cot that was beside the bed and something twisted in his heart. Memories, dark and shadowed, seemed to try to push up through the years. A dark contrast to this mother who loved her two children with all her heart, who would protect them from harm at any cost. Whereas his own mother hadn't given a damn, had caused harm to her children through sheer apathy and neglect.

Suddenly aware of Zoe's gaze on him, he pushed the thoughts away. This was not about him. 'We'll leave you to rest,' he said softly, and he and Zoe exited the room.

Once in the hallway, she stopped and placed a hand on his arm. 'Are you OK? I know you're worried about Prisha and I think her situation might be triggering you, reminding you of your childhood.'

Matt stared at her, realised that this was the consequence of sharing confidences, that people could read you, see into your mind and heart, and he didn't like it. Right now he couldn't afford to be triggered, couldn't afford to let emotion impact the work he needed to do. And so he did not need Zoe, or the compassion in her eyes. Zoe brought out emotion in him and that was dangerous; he'd already known that, but now the danger was magnified. He had to be on his game, in control.

'I'm fine. Truly, Zoe. Right now we need to focus on what needs to be done. Also, I spoke with Edwina. We can stay here. They've set up fold-up beds in separate rooms. I think that's more appropriate.'

'Of course.'

He nodded. 'Right, we'll meet later and I'll let you know what the lawyer says.'

Two days later Zoe stirred the enormous pan of soup she was making for the following day's lunch, glanced at the clock and saw it was past eleven. But cooking helped her, relaxed her and distracted her from the hurt she was feeling. Irrational hurt, she told herself.

Only it didn't feel that way; it just hurt. The fact that since they'd got here Matt had

completely withdrawn from her. She understood he was working flat out for both Prisha
and Chaneth, knew too that he was investi-
gating the legality of Prisha's marriage, was
searching for witnesses who would attest to
her husband's violence. But these facts were
delivered in their evening meetings with Edwina and Prisha and then he would disappear
to his room, situated at the other end of the
orphanage from her own.

She'd thought after their beach run, after
all they'd shared in Burati, that Matt had
changed, was opening up. Yet since they'd
got here he'd closed down. He also looked
terrible, or as terrible as it was possible for
Matt to look, with dark circles under his eyes.

Zoe looked down into the orange swirl of
the soup. Right. It was daft of her to think
that Matt would voluntarily talk to her. And
it was stupid and petty of her to be hurt that
he wasn't. But what she could do was at least
make sure he ate properly. She found a bowl
and ladled some of the soup in. He'd worked
through dinner and she had the feeling he'd
skipped lunch. She quickly heated up a *roti*,
placed it on a plate and found a small tray.

A few minutes later she approached his
door, wondered belatedly if he might be
asleep. She slowed, stopped outside the door

to listen and frowned. Perhaps he was on the phone—she could hear the rumble of a voice, a mutter, a murmur that sounded distressed and then there was a cry, a cry of pain, horror, revulsion, hurt. It pierced the air and without thought she placed the tray on the floor, pushed the door open and went in. Matt was sitting up in bed, his eyes open, though she sensed he was still in the grip of his nightmare. His eyes were wide, his skin pale, his dark hair mussed. But it was his expression that tore at her heartstrings—there was fear there and she'd never once seen Matt afraid.

'Matt?' She kept her voice gentle, didn't want to spook him, even as her mind raced with questions. She perched on the bed next to him, put out a tentative hand and laid it on his shoulder, felt the clamminess of his skin, saw the twist of the sheets and wondered how long his nightmare had been. 'It's OK. It was a dream.' But clearly not any dream, not to go by the haunted look on his face. Then he blinked, a long slow blink, and she could almost see the process of pulling himself together begin.

He shifted away from her, swung his legs out of bed. 'I'm fine. I'll be back in a second.' He tugged on a pair of jeans and left the room, returned a few minutes later, towel in hand, his face and torso wet. 'That's better,' he said, remaining standing as he towelled off. 'Sorry. Did I wake you? I must have had a bad dream.' His tone was dismissive; she suspected he was aiming for nonchalance.

'You didn't wake me. I came to bring you some food.' She hesitated. 'That looked like a lot worse than just a bad dream. You were terrified.'

His expression shuttered off as he shrugged. 'That's what bad dreams can do.'

'Do you have bad dreams often?' she asked.

'No. Look, Zoe, I don't really want to talk about it.'

'I get that, but you can't expect me to walk away and pretend it didn't happen. I'm worried about you.'

'Don't be. It's Prisha and Chaneth you need to be worried about.'

'I am worried about them, but you have done everything possible to help them.'

'What if it isn't enough?' His voice was laced with a mix of frustration and fear.

'That is an unanswerable question. But the lawyer said she was cautiously optimistic—and there is nothing more you can do.'

'But maybe there is. Maybe I've missed something.'

'And maybe you are making yourself ill. You're not even eating.'

'I am…' He broke off.

'So please at least eat the soup and *roti*.' She rose and went to get the tray. 'If you get ill you won't be able to help anyone, and then what will happen?'

CHAPTER THIRTEEN

MATT MET HER GAZE, looked down at the soup and realised Zoe was right. He hadn't eaten since breakfast and he did need to eat.

'Thank you,' he said, then placed the tray on the desk and started to eat. The spicy tang of the soup, the smooth texture, offered a comfort and he realised he was in fact ravenous.

Once he'd eaten the last bite he turned, and the words of thanks died on his lips.

'What are you doing?' The question was pointless as he could quite clearly see what she was doing as she smoothed the twist of sheets on the bed, shook out the blanket and calmly climbed underneath.

'I'm staying here. I am not leaving you alone in case you have another nightmare.'

'I...' What was he supposed to do now? The only way to get Zoe to leave would be to pick her up and carry her out. He supposed he could go and sit at his desk and try to work, could read and reread the emails from the lawyer to see if there was anything he or she had missed. Problem was he'd already done that and perhaps that was what had triggered his nightmare.

He looked at the bed again. Zoe lay there, eyes closed, clearly feigning sleep, but she looked so peaceful, so calm, so right there in his bed that he shrugged. There could be no harm in simply lying next to her.

Letting out a sigh, he climbed into the bed next to her, made sure to keep a gap between them and stared up at the ceiling, felt his eyes close and wondered if he should try and stay awake. But surely the dream wouldn't recur… the same night. Not now he was properly awake.

How wrong he was—he sank back in the dream, only now the dream was muddled. Prisha's husband was there. So was Prisha, cradling her baby, Tomas by her side. The husband approached but, instead of it being Prisha, it was the fuzzy outline of a different woman who handed the baby over. And Matt was standing in a corner, powerless, watching as though it were a movie, popcorn by his side. Then he saw the baby wasn't Adam; it was Peter—he didn't know how he knew, but he did, and he let out a roar…cried out his brother's name.

And then he heard a voice…a familiar voice rife with worry but also with care, a soothing voice. 'Matt. It's a dream. It's OK now.' A tendril of hair tickled his face and the familiarity of it brought him to the present, to reality.

He opened his eyes fully and sat up, looked into Zoe's wide green eyes. 'That sounded rough,' she said.

'I'm fine.' He blinked the lingering images away.

'No. You are not fine.' Her hand was back on his arm, her touch a comfort. 'I wish you'd talk to me. I want to help.'

He stared at her face, saw such genuine compassion, and he recalled everything she'd done in the past days. 'You've already helped so much, Zoe. You've been a rock for all the kids. I've seen how much Ravima and Nimali look up to you. You've kept them occupied and you've provided food and you've really been there for Prisha. I've seen how you've looked after Adam so Prisha can focus on Tomas. And she trusts you.'

'I've wanted to do everything I've done. I've got pretty attached to all these kids. But I'm not thinking about them now. I'm thinking about you. I don't even know who Peter is.' Now her other hand was on his other arm and she had shifted closer.

Looking at her, he knew he owed her an explanation. Zoe hadn't had to come here, to give him soup, hadn't had to stay. Plus, how could he not tell the truth about Peter? He wouldn't deny his brother's existence... wouldn't lie to her.

'Peter was my brother, my little brother.' Sadness, guilt, pain hoarsened his voice.

'What happened to him?' Her hand tightened round his arm.

'He died. He was five months old and he died. Apparently he was always sickly. He got pneumonia and my parents...our parents... didn't do anything. A neighbour ended up taking him into hospital. But it was too late. The neighbour told the social workers about me as well and that's when I was taken into care.' He looked at her, his whole being and soul bleak. 'He died. I lived. I should have saved him, helped him, done something.'

'No.' The word was anguished and she moved closer to him now. 'You were five years old.'

'It doesn't matter.'

'You were too young.' She moved closer to him, so close, put her arm round him, and he tried to force the rigidity of his body to relax, to accept the comfort she was offering, a comfort he knew he didn't deserve. 'You mustn't carry this responsibility, the burden of grief and guilt. It is tragic what happened to Peter, to that tiny, frail baby. But it's not your fault.'

'But if I'd acted differently he may have lived.'

'And so you wish you could turn the clock back, and you go through a litany of ifs and buts and if-onlys and what-ifs. I promise you I understand how that feels. But I know that you have no need to feel it.'

He glanced at her, knew with bone-deep knowledge the words came from empathy, not sympathy. 'But you do?'

Zoe shook her head. 'This isn't about me.'

'No. This is about us. You and me.' And the tragedy was that there was nothing more he could tell her about Peter, because he didn't remember him, saw him only in dreams. And whilst he truly appreciated Zoe's belief in him, her attempt to lift his burden of guilt, he knew no words could do that. The very fact he couldn't recall his brother's existence told him there was something wrong with him. But perhaps he could help Zoe, because he could see the pain in her eyes, a depth of guilt that mirrored his own. 'Tell me. Let me help.'

She took a deep breath and now he placed an arm on her shoulders, rested it lightly there, could feel her tension.

'I was never like Beth,' she began. 'I wanted my parents' attention and so I shouted, screamed, did anything I could to get it. At sixteen I took it up a few notches—I turned full-on rebel. I took up alcohol, started partying—I even ended up in a police cell. Even that didn't get their attention. They sent a neighbour to get me out. Then I fell in love, or thought I did.

'Tom came from a super-rich background—he was slumming it at some party I was at. But we had a bond. His parents were caught up in their own lives—they'd got him nannies and boarding schools. He said he sometimes wondered if they even remembered his name. Anyway, I took him on the path of rebellion with me. I ended up taking him to a party I'd heard about... We gatecrashed it. At first I thought it was perfect, much older kids and, oh, so cool. Then I saw there were hard drugs circulating. That was too far even for me. I went to find Tom and found him with another girl. We had a row. I told him it was over. He swore the girl had kissed him and he was drunk, told me he loved me, but I wouldn't listen. I stormed off and left him there.' Tears glistened in her green eyes now. 'I never saw him again. He took an accidental overdose and he died.'

The words were so stark they jolted through him, her pain his own as he imagined the guilt and regret that would have seared through her.

'Oh, Zoe…' He gathered her into his arms and held her. Knew and understood how impossible it was to live with a scenario where the what-ifs must saw through her brain. 'It wasn't your fault.'

'But there are so many different ways it could have played out. If I'd been more understanding—I knew Tom was drunk. I should have *made* him come with me. I shouldn't have broken up with him, then maybe he wouldn't have taken the drugs. I should have called Beth to come and get me, not a taxi. Beth would have gone and got Tom. I should never have been so pathetic as to rebel in the first place, just for my parents' attention.'

He held her tighter. 'I get it,' he said. 'I truly do. But you can't torture yourself with all those what-ifs. If you'd known what would happen, of course you would have acted differently, but none of us can predict the future—you could not have known. Tom chose to take those drugs, and of course he didn't deserve to die but it is not your fault. But I get that it seems as though it is. And I'm sorry.' He stroked her back. 'And I'm sorry for your loss. You lost your first love and even without everything else that must have been traumatic. Did you go to counselling at all? Talk to anyone about how you felt?'

Zoe shook her head. 'Beth was amazing and really there for me but somehow counselling felt too…scary. And almost self-indulgent. I mean, I didn't die, Tom did. And if I was feeling guilty, then I think I figured I deserved it.'

'Do you still think that?'

Zoe moved backwards so she could see him properly and then shifted so they were both sitting, backs against the wall, his arm still around her shoulders. 'Yes, I suppose I do.'

'No.' He shook his head. 'You don't deserve to feel guilty. Sad, of course—it is tragic that Tom died so young. Regret that you couldn't stop the tragedy. Absolutely. But not guilt.'

'Then surely the same goes for you.' Her voice was small. 'Only even more so. You were a child.'

The words arrested him and he looked at her. If he was so sure he was right about Zoe, then he couldn't refuse to look at his own tragedy through the same lens. And he tried to do just that, but how could he absolve himself? Peter had been an innocent. His baby brother had had no choice in his destiny. Tom, however, had to take some responsibility for his own tragic death. He had chosen to stay at the party, chosen to take the drugs. Zoe had done nothing wrong; she hadn't known what Tom would do…hadn't known he was in trouble. Matt would have seen his brother, must have known he needed help. At the very least he should remember Peter; the very fact he couldn't hinted that he simply hadn't cared, just as his parents hadn't.

But Zoe… He looked at her. He didn't want her to carry this burden for ever.

'I've got an idea.' It meant leaving the orphanage for a bit, but it should be OK. He knew logically Prisha's husband would not try a forced entry. Not with the amount of security that surrounded the building. Plus, there was a guard on Prisha's door. Plus, he knew Chaneth was also outside Prisha's door.

'It is always best if someone is watching the guard,' he'd explained with a serious expression on his face. 'People are corruptible. I will keep watch and so too will the others.'

Matt climbed out of bed and held out a hand to pull her up. 'Grab a jacket,' he instructed.

'Where are we going?' she asked as they emerged outside the orphanage, into the early hours of the day with dawn tiptoeing into the sky with fingers of pink and orange. The village was awakening, the clang and clatter of cooking pots, a stream of workers headed for the tea plantation, and early tea vendors plying their trade.

'To lay an offering at a shrine,' he said. 'This place is home to one of the most sacred things in Sri Lanka: an ancient tree grown from the saplings of a tree that sheltered Buddha himself. It is thousands of years old and I think…maybe if you go and lay some flowers for Tom it may help a little. It would be a chance to say sorry that things didn't work out differently.' He stopped and held her hands in his. 'I want somehow to lighten your load of guilt.'

'And what about you?'

'I'll lay some flowers for Peter as well.' Take the chance to say sorry that he hadn't saved him.

She looked up at him and he saw the slight frown in her eyes; quickly he started walking again. This was about Zoe now. He didn't want to hear any more reassurances about himself; his guilt was his to bear and could not be lightened. But he hoped, truly hoped, that Zoe's could be.

They paused at a flower seller close to the shrine and then joined the people making their way forward.

As Matt laid the flowers down he looked at the tree and sensed the awe and reverence in which it was held. He thought of Peter, his baby brother. 'I wish I had saved you, wish I had been a better brother. I'm sorry I wasn't.'

He felt a sense of comfort, hoped his brother could forgive him. Wished that he could forgive himself.

He stepped aside and watched as Zoe crouched down and put her flowers next to his, saw her close her eyes, heard her murmur, 'I'm sorry, Tom. But thank you for being there for me, for being my partner in crime, the person who understood me. I'm sorry I couldn't prevent your death. More sorry than I can ever say. But I will try and honour your memory.'

She rose, her face pale, but he thought he could see a sense of peace that hadn't been there before. Matt knew this wouldn't chase

all her demons away, but he hoped it would
be a start.

'Thank you,' she said as they walked away.
'That was… I'm glad we did that. I feel…
lighter.'

'I'm glad.'

He smiled at her. 'We should get back in
time for breakfast,' he said. 'And from now
on I promise not to push you away. We're in
this together.'

CHAPTER FOURTEEN

'WE WON! WE WON! We won!'

Zoe could still hardly believe it; happiness bubbled inside her along with a relief so intense she could almost cry.

A happiness shared by the entire orphanage—the past days the tension had escalated with everyone increasingly on edge. But it had been Matt who had been the calmest of them all. He'd worked indefatigably, had called in an additional lawyer, but had also promised if the case went against them it wouldn't be the end of it all.

But he had also managed to cheer people up, to keep spirits high, and Zoe had done her best to help with that.

And now Prisha was safe and so were her children. For the first time in days Tomas smiled as he watched all the orphans form a conga and dance round the table.

Zoe went to stand by Matt. 'You did it,' she

whispered. 'You saved them.' She understood so much more now why he did what he did. He hadn't been able to save Peter and so now he saved as many other children as he could.

'We saved them,' he said. 'All of us. And it feels good.'

Zoe nodded. 'And now for the celebration dinner.' They'd asked the lawyer to attend as well as the local police superintendent, as Matt wanted to make sure security was maintained for a while. 'I've gone absolutely all out. I've even made sparkling pink lemonade, or something like it. And I've made jackfruit curry, which I know is Prisha's favourite, and a massive chocolate cake for dessert with cardamom ice cream.'

Edwina approached them as she spoke. 'That sounds incredible, Zoe. I just want to thank you both again for everything you've done. The past six days have felt like months. I cannot tell you how grateful we are to you— if she hadn't won this case, I don't know what would have happened to her.'

Six days. For some reason the words prompted a slight sense of panic in Zoe. Why? Her gaze flickered to Matt and the panic upped a bar. Soon it would be time to say goodbye, to move on from this layer of the present to the next. One that did not contain Matt.

One that contained her new business venture and her first step towards a family. A family. Six days. A family. Six days. Oh, Lord. Six days ago…she should have started her period.

'Zoe? Are you OK?'

She looked at Matt. 'Of course. I just remembered I've forgotten the sprinkles for the cupcakes. I'm going to pop out and get some.'

'I'm sure we can manage without sprinkles.'

'Nope. I want them to be perfect. I won't be long.'

As she left her brain raced with anxiety, panic and, she realised, a small sense of anticipation. She had to stay calm; there was no sense in second-guessing anything. The important thing now was to find a pharmacy that sold a super-sensitive pregnancy test. Mission accomplished, she bought the sprinkles she had supposedly left the orphanage for and hurried back.

She entered and forced a smile to her face as Ravima ran across the room to her. 'I've been talking to Ms Vardis, the lawyer, and she has been great. She's going to try and help me.'

Zoe's smile turned to a genuine one, and as she hugged the teenager she determined to put her potential problem from her mind for now. This was a celebration and she wanted to be part of it. 'That is brilliant news. And I know you can do this—follow your dream.' She tugged the sprinkles out of her bag. 'Now I'll just go and put the finishing touches to lunch.'

The next couple of hours passed by in a blur and Zoe was proud of herself that she genuinely enjoyed the lunch, loved seeing the happiness that pervaded the air, the laughter and jokes and, most of all, watching Tomas and Adam and knowing they were safe.

But she kept her gaze averted from Matt, the one brief glimpse she allowed herself too much. He looked so relaxed, so gorgeous, so…Matt, and her tummy swooped and dived at the possibility she was pregnant. With his baby. She closed her eyes briefly, knew with devastating clarity that part of her hoped she was. Not that she expected anything from him; this time she knew he didn't want a family, could understand why he wanted to devote his life to a cause, to helping children.

But maybe… Maybe what? He'd be a part-time father?

Whoa.

She hadn't even done a test yet. But she couldn't help herself—now an impossible dream drifted into her brain like pink-tinted cotton wool. Matt being happy about the baby, saying everything was different now, that he wanted the same things Zoe wanted, that…

'Zoe?'

She blinked, aware of Edwina's concerned face. 'Are you OK?'

'I'm fine.'

She glanced round the table, realised everyone was holding up their sparkling lemonade for a toast, aware too that Matt was studying her expression. Damn, she'd been doing so well. She lifted her glass and smiled. 'To Prisha,' she echoed everyone round the table. 'And a brand-new start.' The words held an extra meaning, and she resisted the telltale urge to touch her stomach.

Two hours later, Matt approached Zoe's room, worry and disquiet churning in his chest as he knocked at the door and entered to her call of, 'Come in.'

'Hey.' Her smile was wary. 'How did it go with the police superintendent?'

'Great. Better than great.' For a second he focused on the conversation he'd just left. 'He's agreed to keep an eye on things and he's agreed to take Chaneth on.'

'You mean to work for the police force?'

'Yup. It's perfect—that way Chaneth can

do good, and he'll know that he isn't born to be a criminal.' He shook his head. 'But that's not why I'm here. I'm worried because I found this.' He handed over the receipt he'd found on the floor whilst clearing up. 'One of the girls must have dropped it but I've no idea who. I wondered if perhaps you had any idea.'

She looked down at the slip of paper, a receipt from a pharmacy for a pregnancy test, then back up at him, her green eyes wide in shock and…something else.

And in that moment clarity dawned in a blinding burst of a truth so obvious he could only marvel at his own foolishness. Had he really believed the receipt had been dropped by one of the orphans?

'It's mine,' Zoe said. The words so brief and yet so massive in their impact.

'But…it can't be.'

'You mean you don't want it to be.'

Of course he didn't. Because this couldn't work. It was all wrong for Zoe, for the baby… History was repeating itself with a mocking vengeance and he couldn't keep the accusation from his tone. 'You said you were on the pill.'

'I am on the pill. I told you I went on it a year ago because I was doing a lot of travelling and it helped if my periods were more regulated.'

His eyes narrowed and suspicion raised its ugly head, spurred on by a sense of impending panic, the knowledge that for a second time he would be found wanting, the fear of failure, the fear of loss. 'Or you decided this was the way to get the family you want. Decided to dispense with Mr Right and cut straight to the chase. Was that it?' Even as the words spewed from his mouth he knew they should remain unspoken, unthought, but that dark panic drove him on. 'And I was the perfect candidate because this time you thought I'd walk away.'

Zoe sat frozen still, the pain etched on her face so raw that Matt would have done anything to take the words back.

'If that is what you believe of me, then the past weeks have been utterly meaningless,' she said. '*Completely* devoid of *any* meaning.' She rose, her face pale, her eyes dark with anger and misery. 'Get out, Matt. I don't want to see you again.'

And he didn't blame her. 'Zoe. I'm sorry. I shouldn't have said that. Any of that.'

'Damn straight you shouldn't have. I would never do that. To you, or to anyone. You knew what I wanted, what my dream is. For a family. I want my baby to have a father who wants him or her. I know that's not what you want and I respect that.' Her voice broke. 'Please leave. Now.'

'No. I can't just leave. This baby…is my baby too.'

She gazed directly into his eyes. 'It doesn't matter—I don't want my baby to have a father who resents its existence, a father who lets it down because he can't commit. So actually, Matt, this time round, this baby is mine. Of course I won't stop you from seeing him or her, but that's it. I know you don't want a family and I will not get in the way of that.' Her voice was still tight with hurt and he didn't know what to do or say to excuse himself, knew too that she was right—he couldn't give her what she wanted. Couldn't risk being a bad parent and a worse husband. 'That's even assuming there is a baby. I was about to do the test when you came in.' She rose. 'I'll let you know.'

Now a confusion of emotion hit him. There was relief that perhaps this wasn't happening, but there was also a sense of sorrow for this baby that they had discussed as if he were real. A sudden longing that things could be different, that he could be Zoe's Mr Right, that they were hoping for a positive result, wanted to welcome the baby into the world together.

But that wasn't for him. It would be self-ish to risk it and yet he knew with bone-deep certainty that if Zoe was pregnant he would risk it. Because, just as it had been four years ago, he could not knowingly neglect his own flesh and blood. Even if he had to fake it to the core, even if he truly felt nothing, his child would never know it.

'I'll wait here. And, Zoe, if you are pregnant, I'm not going anywhere. I won't walk away from my baby. I won't be guilty of neglect.'

Her face softened. 'I understand that. But I won't be trapped in a fake family scenario—we will work out the best way forward. That allows you to carry on your foundation work and gives me a chance to work out how to be a single-parent family.'

'No.'

'Yes. You have made it perfectly clear that you want to prioritise your foundation over a family.'

'That is not the reason I don't want a family.'

Her forehead creased in a frown of scepti-cism. 'I don't understand.'

'I don't want a family because I can't risk it. I can't risk that I am like my parents, genetically programmed to be a bad father.' The words were imbued with both bitterness and sorrow.

Now sorrow touched her features, and her mouth was a circle of shock as she shook her head so vigorously her ponytail weaved and bobbed. 'You are nothing like your parents— I've seen you with all these kids—you are nothing like them. You care.'

'But I didn't care about Peter.'

'Of course you did. Maybe you couldn't save him, but that's because you were a child.'

'Then why can't I even remember him?' The question was wrenched from him as pain and guilt twisted his insides. 'I only know he existed because a foster carer asked me about him, and I didn't know what she was talking about. I don't remember anything about him, seeing him, hearing him, holding him, try-ing to feed him, nothing. And there's every chance that's because I didn't bother, didn't care. Just like my parents.'

'Or perhaps your brain has blocked those years out because of how bad they were. To protect you. The blame for what happened to Peter lies squarely with your parents.' The fierceness in her voice was rock solid.

'With the two human beings who made me. Their genes run rife inside me and maybe all I can do is control them. What if I have a baby and I feel nothing for him or her? That's too big a risk for me to knowingly take. But if you are pregnant, then I will not walk away, and the baby will be the most important thing in my life. Even if I fake every emotion—that baby will never feel neglected by me. And I am not going anywhere.' He stopped. 'I just need you to know that before you do the test.'

Zoe came towards him, reached up and fleetingly touched his cheek with her hand. 'Thank you. I don't know what the answer is, but if I am pregnant at least this time we've been honest with each other. I'll go and do the test now.'

She picked up a box from the table and left the room and he started to pace.

Zoe stared down at the test, knowing this would be the longest three minutes of her life, waiting and watching to see if the pink lines would appear. Her head felt fuzzy, her whole body roiled with emotion. Dread mixed with hope; how could she hope that this was positive? This was not the plan. She wanted a family, had plotted and planned a whole campaign to have her family with Mr Right.

Not with Matt.

Matt was supposed to be fun and uncomplicated. But it hadn't been, had it? Sure, some of it had been fun, but some of it had been real. Gritty and uncomfortable and real. Sex hadn't even been part of the equation the last few days; instead they'd been focused on the children, the case and their own pasts. They'd shared so much more than a bed. Enough so that he should never have hurled the accusations he'd hurled, but now she understood they stemmed from panic rather than belief. Her heart cracked anew at the demons he carried on his shoulder. How could he believe that he was anything like his parents?

One minute down.

Yet there was a twisted honour in his refusal to risk a family. Surely that showed him he was nothing like his parents. If she was pregnant now that would be proof to him that he was a family man—because of course he'd love the baby. She knew that with every fibre of her being. Just as she knew she would love this baby with all her heart. But how would they manage? What would they do?

Another minute down.

Now she cleared her mind of all thought, sat with her eyes closed and then the timer of her phone pinged. In that moment she knew that she wanted those lines to appear, wanted the baby. Wanted Matt's baby.

Because she loved him.

Shock jolted her, along with a sense of horror. How could she have been so stupid? He didn't tick the most important box of all. He wasn't Mr Right, but she loved him anyway. How shallow did that make her? How could she have fallen for someone who didn't want a family? That made her...ridiculous.

Take a deep breath. She needed to stay calm whilst she assessed the extent of the disaster. This was not love—this was some sort of hormonal surge brought on by anxiety over the test result, mixed with the stupid attraction, mixed with the tension of the past days. That was it—this was like a schoolgirl crush on the hero of the hour. Nothing more. It couldn't be anything more. But it was. She loved the man with all the depths of her heart and soul.

So it was time to open her eyes and see the results.

Matt halted midstride as the door opened and his gaze flew to Zoe's face; he tried to read her expression. Shell shock mixed with sadness.

'As it turns out there was no need to panic. I'm not pregnant. The test was negative.'

He waited for relief to hit but it didn't come. He tried to analyse how he felt, but couldn't— it was as though the emotions had all surged together and merged into a bleak sense of loss. For an imaginary future that would now not come to pass.

'That's g...' His tongue stumbled on the word and he forced it out. 'Good news.'

'It doesn't feel like good news.' She took a deep breath, stepped towards him. 'For either of us. I know you would be a good dad. This would have been your chance to see that, to see I'm right. I understand why you're scared—I would be too, but you need to believe in yourself.'

'I do believe in myself.' Only the words sounded hollow, as hollow as he felt inside. 'I believe in my company, in my skill set, in my foundation.' And he had the money in the bank, the trappings of wealth, the awards and, most important, a record of the good his foundation had done to prove it.

She shook her head. 'I don't mean any of that. I mean believe in your ability to love and be loved. You have that in you.'

Only he didn't. He looked down into her beautiful green eyes and he wanted to weep.

He wished, wished with all his heart, that he could be her Mr Right, give her everything she wanted in life, what she most wanted in life. A family. But he couldn't—he was a bad risk. A husk of a man, empty inside. And she deserved her happy ending. He wouldn't stand in the way of that.

'Only I don't. You need to start your quest for a real Mr Right, a man who you know will be a great dad, whose dream is a family. So it is good news.' It had to be. 'This way you...we can resume our normal lives as planned.' The words were leaden and he tried for some form of uplift. 'The next layer. That's a good thing.'

'Yes.' She gave a small laugh, the sound an almost strangled gurgle, a travesty of her true laugh. 'Funnily enough today is the last day of the festival, the day the relic is returned to its golden box in the temple. I suppose that's fitting.' She met his gaze directly. 'But it doesn't feel like that. Is this how your relationships work? Because this doesn't feel fun or uncomplicated.'

She was right. It didn't. It felt desolating.

'No, it doesn't. My type of relationship didn't work for us. Maybe it couldn't between us, maybe we had too much history, but somewhere along the way we ended up drifting from the shallow end to the deep and we need to get out now before we both drown.'

Pain touched her face and then she nodded. 'You're right.' She paused. 'I don't want the children to feel there's anything wrong so I suggest I leave tomorrow—I'll explain my sister needs me.' Another deep breath. 'When we see each other next I truly hope it won't be awkward.'

He wished he could think of something—anything—to say. But there was nothing... zip, *nada*. So he turned and walked slowly from the room.

One month later

Matt tried to keep his heart from pounding his ribcage as he entered the building that housed social services in the area of London where he'd been born. He walked to the reception desk and announced his name and was told to take a seat. Five minutes later a young woman entered the waiting room.

'Matt? Hi, I'm Janine. We spoke on the phone. It's good to meet you.'

'And you.'

'Come through to my office.'

Once seated, he glanced around, appreciated the touches to the institutionalised room—the row of cacti on the windowsill, the personalised mug on the desk.

'Before I give you the files, can I check that you are sure this is what you want to do?'

'Yes, it is. I've spoken with the counsellor and I do want to go ahead.'

'You understand these files detail the circumstances around your being taken into care.'

'Yes. I understand.'

'OK.' She unlocked a drawer and pulled out a pile of files. 'You can't take these away, but you can take notes and obviously you can come back on later dates. Take your time. If you need a break, give me a call and I'll lock the files up. I've booked the room for the whole day as you requested.'

'Thank you.' Once Janine had gone Matt looked at the files. This was the right thing to do. His whole life, he'd believed the past didn't matter. Or so he'd said. But it did. The past affected the present and the future. And now he needed to try and understand it. Why he couldn't remember those early years, why he couldn't remember his brother, what those years had been like.

He could taste the bitter tang of fear in his mouth, but he knew this was important.

Knew he had to face his past to have any hope of a future. The future he wanted.

Skin clammy, heart pounding, he opened the top file and started to read.

Zoe looked up from unpacking boxes in her newly rented London apartment and smiled at her sister.

'I came to see how you were settling in.' Beth watched as Zoe rose to her feet and indicated round the room.

'I'm not settled yet. Once I get everything unpacked, I'm sure it will be OK.'

Only she wasn't. Nothing felt OK. She missed Matt, more than she thought it possible to miss anyone. She missed the feel of his hand around hers, his smell, his smile, the sound of his voice. She missed telling him things, trivial and important, she missed waking up next to him, safely cocooned in his arms. She missed all of him; worst of all, it didn't seem to be getting any better. However hard she worked.

Oh, she wouldn't give up; she'd spent the last few nights going over her business plans, contacting street-market organisers but any sense of excitement felt dulled.

But it would pass.

'Actually,' Beth said, 'I came here to talk to you, and Dylan has gone to see Matt.'

'Is he OK?' What if he'd stopped eating again? What if the nightmares were back? What if something had happened to one of the kids he cared about or there'd been a stock market crash or…?

'No. I don't think he is. And I don't think you are either, so I wanted to say sorry. From Dylan and me. We should never have let David give you that gift. It wasn't fair on either of you.'

'I don't think you had any choice in the matter. And what happened between Matt and me is not your fault. It's ours and we'll both get over it. I need to put it behind me and move on.'

'Why?' Beth frowned. 'I don't mean to pry but I don't get it. You're both miserable.'

'It doesn't matter.'

Her sister's frown deepened. 'Do you love him, Zoe?'

'Yes.' The word was a wail. 'But I don't want to. Matt doesn't do love.'

'Are you sure? Maybe he hasn't said the words, but how has he acted?'

Zoe thought about the answer to that. Recalled the time he'd held the cushion for her to punch, then listened to her talk about her family. The way he'd listened to her talk about Tom, taken her to the shrine. The things he'd shared with her. The way he'd held her close and safe. But Matt had also cared about Prisha and Chaneth and the orphans. But that was different. Because Matt had also confided in her, shared things he had never shared before.

'But none of that matters anyway. Because Matt doesn't want a family.'

Beth frowned. 'Are you sure he doesn't?'

'Yes. But I do. In fact I had—I have—a plan. I'm going to find a man, a good, decent man to settle down with and…' She broke off as she saw Beth's face. 'OK. I get that plan isn't going to work until I'm over Matt. But I will get over him. And if not, then I'll become a single parent. I'll adopt or use a donor or…something.'

Beth stepped towards her and pulled her into a hug, before releasing her and gesturing to the sofa. 'I'm making us some tea and then I want to say a few things.'

Five minutes later, cradling the steaming mug, she looked closely at Zoe.

'I get why you want a family; you want what we never had. And I understand that. I want that too and, yes, Dylan does want a family as well. But if he didn't, it wouldn't be a deal-breaker. It never would have been. I wouldn't stop loving him. Or if one of us can't have kids we wouldn't break up. We'd figure it out. But I'd rather grow old with Dylan, with the man I love and who loves me, and not have kids than not have Dylan.' She put her mug down, reached out and covered Zoe's hand. 'I get it's different for everyone and only you know your priorities, but please promise me you'll think about what I've said.'

Zoe stared at her sister, her lovely, wise, beautiful sister. 'I promise,' she said softly. Once her sister had left she sat down, her head awhirl. Got back up and grabbed her jacket.

Twenty minutes later she was knocking at David and Manisha's door, relieved when Manisha pulled it open and smiled in welcome.

'Zoe. How lovely to see you.'

'I am so sorry to drop by unannounced. I wondered if I can have a quick word with you and David.'

'Of course. Come in.'

Having refused all offers of refreshment, Zoe sat opposite the couple, touched by how close they sat together on the sofa, the way Manisha held her husband's hand as if she needed to keep him close.

'I…well, I was wondering why you gave Matt and me the trip to Burati.'

David studied her face closely. 'Because I saw the way he looked at you, when you and Beth came into the hospital room. He couldn't hide how he felt. He may have been able to hide it from you, maybe even from himself, but that look said it all. I am a statistician. I weighed up the odds. If the two of you had gone your separate ways after the wedding he may never have figured out how he felt about you. If the two of you spent more time together he might. I was trying to help the odds. I've always had a lot of time for Matt— he's a good man who helped my son. I wanted to pay my debt in case I didn't come back.'

'I'm very glad you did,' Zoe said. 'And thank you. For everything.'

Three days later

Matt glanced down at his post and froze— amongst the bills and circulars there was a card addressed in a hand he recognised instantly, a sprawling, loopy hand. Zoe. He picked it up and carefully opened it, saw a gold-edged invitation inside.

*You are cordially invited
to a food-tasting session
Food cooked by Zoe Trewallen*

Matt's heart leapt, even though he knew perhaps it shouldn't—presumably this was an olive branch, a way for them to meet in public, with plenty of other people. A way to pave the way for future inevitable meetings.

Well, that was fine with him. He'd accept an olive branch; it didn't change his own plans. And he'd get to see her... Now his heart did a small somersault only to plunge downward in panic. What if she brought a date? What if she'd started the process of finding Mr Right? Maybe this was her way of showing him.

Well, he'd just have to pick him up and throw him out by the seat of his pants. No! He'd have to suck it up, remind himself he wanted what was best for Zoe.

He looked back down at the invitation, noted it didn't have an RSVP option. Should he call her? Text her? Or maybe it was a sign she didn't want to know. But what did that mean?

He needed to get a grip.

Three days later

Zoe looked round the room, focused on the details, wondered again if this was a good idea. It certainly ran against her MO—she wasn't running away, even though right now part of her was telling her to do exactly that. But she wouldn't. Not this time. Her professional eye double-checked that the hotplates were working, that the food she cooked with such care would remain at the right temperatures.

That was always provided there was anyone to eat it.

As if on cue the door opened and she forced herself to remain still as relief coursed through her as Matt walked in. She would not make a fool of herself and launch herself at his chest. But, oh, how she wanted to—wanted to touch, smell, hug, hold. Instead she settled for a small smile as he looked around and then towards her.

'I didn't expect to be the first one here.'

'Um…you aren't. Well, you are, but you're also the last.'

'I don't understand.'

'I know it was a bit of a prevarication, but it wasn't an actual lie. It is a taster session.' She waved her hand at the hotplate. 'But you're the only guest. I thought… I don't know what I thought. OK. I wanted to talk to you, so I guess I tricked you.'

To her relief his face relaxed into a smile. 'That's completely fair enough. I haven't got the best track record for talking. But for the record I would have come. Definitely,' he added.

'Really?'

'Really. I promise. I'd like to talk to you too.'

There was no hint of a lack of sincerity in his face and she risked a tentative smile in return.

'You would?' Was that bad or good? She had no idea. 'I made us cocktails,' she settled for. 'Mojitos.'

'The very first cocktail we ever had. On our first date.' He studied her expression, clearly wondering at the significance.

'Yes.' She gestured towards the food. 'I've made food that's been important in our lives. Fish and chips. The fish cooked in a Brighton batter, the chips in mini cones. A vegetable phall, *masala dosa*. A whole selection.'

She handed him his cocktail and gestured to the table she'd laid with such care.

'Is it OK if I talk first?' she asked.

'Of course.'

'I wasn't really sure where to begin. That's when I decided on the food journey. We began with that first date, those mojitos. And for six months we were happy. Weren't we? Just you and me.'

'Yes,' he said quietly. 'We were.'

'And then I got pregnant and I was so very happy. I hadn't realised until then how much I wanted a family, how much my own upbringing had affected me. I also saw the baby as my chance to somehow start again after Tom. It felt like fate was giving me a chance to atone, to do something positive. Give life.' She sipped her drink, welcomed the tang of the lime and the sweetness of the rum. 'But you didn't know any of that.'

'And you didn't know anything about my background, about my parents or Peter.' He reached out as if to cover her hand and then pulled back.

'No, so I didn't realise how scared and panicked you were.'

'I decided that the best thing I could do was what I was good at. Make money. For the baby, because I thought if I couldn't give him love, then at least I could make sure he was never hungry—that he'd always have everything money could buy. Then when we lost the baby I was devastated. It all mixed up in my head with Peter's death and the nightmares came back. I didn't want you to know.'

'So you started sleeping in the spare room and in my grief all I could think about was having another baby. I became fixated with having a family. I lost sight of…us.'

He shook his head. 'We lost sight of us. And then you left. I told myself it was all for the best. My whole life I had felt empty, no matter how successful I was, whatever I achieved. Until I met you. And then I felt it all. All the feelings and I couldn't cope. When you left, I almost welcomed the emptiness, craved it, told myself it was better than all the hurt and pain.'

'And I came up with my new plan, the only way to have a family without you. I think I knew I could never feel for anyone else how I felt about you so I just thought about having a baby, two babies, and what a great parent I would be and how I'd find the best possible dad.' She took a deep breath. 'I was missing the point.'

'What was the point?'

'You and me. Us. We were important. I know you would have been a wonderful dad to our baby. I truly believe that. But that wasn't meant to be. And I understand why you were terrified, and I understand…I truly do now…why you don't want to take the risk.' She took a deep breath. 'And it doesn't make any difference.' Taking her courage in both hands, she looked at him. 'I love you, Matt. I'm not expecting you to reciprocate or any-thing. But I want you to know I love you. Just you. On your own. You are enough for me. I don't need a package deal. Just you.'

She rose hurriedly to her feet, suddenly not wanting to see his face. 'Please don't say anything. I don't want or need you to. I just wanted you to know that.' Because his whole life he'd never been enough for anyone: his parents had been indifferent, his foster carers had seen him as a job and she'd seen him as a vehicle to a family. 'I'll get the food.' Even assuming he wanted to eat it.

Matt sat transfixed in his seat, then half rose to follow her and then sank back onto the chair. His whole being felt alive, buzzed with joy and happiness and a whole plethora of feelings he couldn't even identify. Until it occurred to him that Zoe had put it all out there, and then he rose at rocket speed and strode over to her, giddy with happiness.

'Zoe.'

'Yes.'

'Turn around. Please.'

She did, though her eyes wouldn't meet his and gently he tipped her chin up.

'I love you too.' The words fell so naturally from his lips, felt so right, so glorious, so steeped in history and yet so unique to them. 'With all my heart. You are my bright shining star and I love you.'

'Really? I don't want you to say it because it's what I want to hear.'

'I'm saying it because I mean it. I love you.' How to prove it? 'Look.' He reached into his jacket pocket. 'I even brought this today. If it seemed right, I was going to give it to you.'

She took the paper and started to read and he saw her eyes mist over.

He'd written it with such hope in his heart, a hope that had now been answered beyond his dreams.

First Date Application:

Dear Zoe
I am writing to apply for a first date. A date where we can talk and I can try to tell you what is in my heart.

Since I saw you last I have missed you more than I can possibly say. I know I don't deserve this, but I wonder if you can give me some time...time to become the man I want to be.

I can wait as long as you want.
Matt

'You don't have to wait at all.' She looked at him and he could see the love glow in her eyes. 'You already are the man I want you to be. You are incredibly kind, caring and decent. You make me laugh, you listen to me, you encourage my dreams. You helped me gain perspective, on my parents, on Tom, and you showed me what charity really means. You're also incredibly gorgeous and make my heart skip a beat every time I see you. I love everything about you exactly as you are, everything.'

'And I love you, Zoe. Because you gave me the courage to face my past. I went to social services and they gave me my files to read.'

'Oh, Matt.' Instantly she was there, by his side, arms looped round him.

'It wasn't pleasant reading. But it gave me some insight into my parents' backgrounds— they had pretty awful childhoods and upbringings themselves and they used alcohol and drugs to forget. I think half the time they probably forgot I was there. It isn't an excuse but at least it makes it slightly more understandable. For those first years I simply existed; I had a primal need to survive so I did. The whole case was a mess; they have no idea how my parents managed to stay under the radar.

'Peter was never even registered. I also managed to track down the neighbour who got Peter to the hospital.' He recalled the meeting; the woman had cried when she'd seen him, told him how sorry she was for turning a blind eye for so long. 'It turns out she didn't even know Peter existed. Nobody did. They must have pretty much given birth at home but who knows how or where? But on the day she called social services in she heard a pounding on the wall and she thinks it was me, because when she came in I said *baby*, but it's possible that until then I didn't really know about Peter.'

'Oh, Matt. That is awful. But if it was you, then you did try to save him.'

He nodded. 'If it was me at least there is a possibility that I tried.' He stopped. 'But even if I didn't...I have realised one day I do want to be a dad, have a baby. With you.'

'You don't have to.'

'I want to. I'm not my parents. I am capable of love—you've shown me that. I love you with all my heart and I know that is real. I love how much you care about people, your family, Prisha, Chaneth. I love how much you care about food. I love your curiosity and your ambitions. I love the way you smile, the feel of your hair, holding your hand. I love that I can talk to you about anything, and I want to have a family with you. You have made me realise I have the capacity to love, and I know

I will love our baby. I want to spend the rest of my life with you, Zoe.'

'As I do with you. I love you, Matt. I didn't know it was possible to be this happy. But I am and we will be. Happy ever after in all the ways that count.'

She stepped forward into his arms, and as he kissed her he knew they would swim the shallows and the deeps together for ever and that he would love this woman until the end of his days.

* * * * *